Matanzas

Garry Ryan

MATANZAS

A Detective Lane Mystery

A NeWest
MYSTERY

COPYRIGHT © GARRY RYAN 2017

LIBRARY AND ARCHIVES CANADA CATALOGUING IN PUBLICATION

Ryan, Garry, 1953–, author
Matanzas / Garry Ryan.

(Detective Lane mystery ; 9)
Issued in print and electronic formats.
IISBN 978-1-988732-09-1 (softcover). — ISBN 978-1-988732-10-7 (EPUB). — ISBN 978-1-988732-11-4 (Kindle)

I. Title. II. Series: Ryan, Garry, 1953– . Detective Lane mystery ; 9

PS8635.Y354M38 2017   C813'.6   C2017-901287-8   C2017-901288-6

Editor for the Board: Leslie Vermeer
Cover and interior design: Natalie Olsen, Kisscut Design
Cover photos: (front) soel/photocase.com, (back) birdys/photocase.com, (page i) Magida El-Kassis/stocksy.com
Author photo: Luke Towers

NeWest Press acknowledges the support of the Canada Council for the Arts, the Alberta Foundation for the Arts, and the Edmonton Arts Council for support of our publishing program. We acknowledge the financial support of the Government of Canada through the Canada Book Fund for our publishing activities.

#201, 8540–109 Street
Edmonton, Alberta T6G 1E6
780.432.9427
NEWEST PRESS www.newestpress.com

No bison were harmed in the making of this book.
Printed and bound in Canada

For my family

CAST OF CHARACTERS

Lane's Family

Alexandra – Christine's half sister

Alison – Christine's mother and Paul Lane's sister who lived in the polygamist community of Paradise

Arthur Merali – an accountant and Lane's spouse

Christine Lane – Paul's niece and mother to Indiana

Daniel Lane – Christine's husband and professional camera operator

Linda Law – Daniel's sister

Lola and John Law – Daniel's parents

Matthew Merali – Arthur's nephew

Paul Lane – veteran homicide detective with Calgary Police Service

Sam – family dog

Lane's Colleagues

Anna – computer/cyber expert in a relationship with Nigel

Cameron Harper – Calgary Deputy Chief and Lane's former police partner

Dr. Colin Weaver (aka Fibre) – head of Forensic Crime Scene Unit

Jean – executive secretary to the Calgary Chief Constable

Jim Simpson – Calgary Chief Constable

Keely Saliba – former partner of Paul Lane who now works in Ottawa with the RCMP

Lori – secretary and quilter who runs the CPS homicide office

Nebal – CPS technology specialist

Nigel Li – homicide detective with the CPS who often works with Lane

Stephen Brown – Crown Prosecutor

Tommy Pham – Paul Lane's lawyer

Cuba Connections

Angella – Havana tour guide

Brett Mara (aka Livingston) – health care professional at Bow Valley Seniors' Residence

Camille Mara (nee Desjardin) – Brett's spouse

Christy Mackenzie – cousin to Camille Mara

Colin Anderson – Jamey's father

Deylis Sanchez – detective with the Cuban police and singer

Hector – Deylis' driver

Jamey Anderson – boy from Toronto on the Havana tour
Omar – moto volqueta driver
Robert North – Camille's friend
Sonja – Brett's Cuban wife
Sylvie – French tourist
Vlad – Cuban cab driver

Calgary Connections
Anita, Aunt Rose and Neville Po – Ayah's relatives
Ayah – resident at Floral Gardens Seniors Residence
Ben Bertoulli – Calgary lawyer
Bill Rogerson – MLA, Solicitor General and Minister of Public Security
Blair and Ronnie – East Coast cowboys
Carlo Tuda – owner of Carlo's Calzones food truck
Colleen – manager at Bow Valley Seniors' Residence
Cora – resident at Bow Valley Seniors' Residence
Cori Pierce – serial killer spouse of Professor Pierce
Donna – Paul Lane's neighbour
Ella – Gloria's niece
FKs or FOBKs – gang
FOBs – gang
Freddy McQuade – friend of Walter Riley
Gloria – childhood neighbour of Paul Lane
Laura Mancuzi – manager at Floral Gardens Seniors Residence
Laura and Shauday – coworkers at Bow Valley Seniors' Residence
Linda – Walter's daughter
Lisa – parole officer in Calgary
Marvin – Walter's roommate
MCSC – **Mi Casa Su Casa** – US based corporation specializing
    in facilities for seniors
Nina and Fernando – high school friends of Paul Lane
Penny – caregiver for Walter Riley at Bow Valley Seniors' Residence
Professor Pierce – serial killer shot and killed by Paul Lane
Robbie VanLeenan – former son-in-law to Walter Riley
Sean Pike – former CPS member and organized crime boss
Terri – coffee kiosk owner on Stephen Avenue Mall
Uncle Tran – recurring character and owner of the Lucky Elephant
    Restaurant
Walter (Wally) Riley – resident at Bow Valley Seniors' Residence

chapter 1

Lane kept his elbows tucked against his rib cage. Arthur looked out the window on one side. An Acadian oil-rig worker sat on the other side of Lane. His biceps were thigh sized and he weighed at least three hundred pounds. Across the aisle from them, Christine sat with Indiana on her lap. Dan looked out the window where the world was white cloud below and blue sky above. Matt slept open mouthed and snored. The jet engines were a constantly reassuring hum.

Lyle, the mountain, pushed back his Flames ball cap and asked, "Your buddy there said you were going to a wedding?"

"Yes, our niece is getting married." Lane looked to his right and up. At six feet, he was dwarfed by Lyle.

"They love Canadians in Cuba. I got married down here. My wife works on one of the resorts."

"Which one?"

"Barceló."

"I think we're at Iberostar."

Lyle nodded, then shifted his weight. Lane's seat bounced forward and back. Lyle said, "I hope my dog is okay."

"Dog?"

"Riley. He's a boxer. Purebred." Lyle pointed at the floor. "He's riding below. The vet gave me some pills so he'd relax. Just hope he slept. He's kind of hyper."

"How did you manage to be born in Acadia, work in Alberta and marry a Cuban?"

Lyle smiled. "Came out west for a job. Ended up working on the rigs. Worked on the rigs down here. Met Antonia.

Took a winter vacation down here, then came back for a few more visits." Lyle held up five fingers. "Bought a house. Her family thinks they've won the lottery because Antonia and I got married. Cubans love Canadians. They don't think much of the Russians and even less of Americans." He poked Lane with a forefinger. "Make sure you tip the people who work at the resort. They work damned hard for very low wages, you know."

"I'll remember that."

"Hey, by the way, what happened to your ear?" Lyle grabbed his own earlobe with a beefy right hand and pointed at Lane's.

Lane lifted his chin. "I went on a domestic disturbance call. The husband was drunk and he was a biter."

"You're a cop?" Lyle looked sideways at Lane, then at Arthur.

"That's right."

Lyle nodded. "You'll be safe in Cuba. The police here do a pretty good job of keeping the tourists safe and happy."

"Good to know."

"Cuba will teach you some new things. It's not the place you've been told about in the media. It's going to delight and disappoint you. It's one of those places you have to see for yourself and make up your own mind about." Lyle closed his mouth, reached into a bag, pulled out a magazine and began to read.

An hour later the jet began its descent to Cuba's Varadero airport. Lane swallowed to equalize the pressure in his ears. Indiana sucked on a bottle of milk with one hand overtop the glass and watched his mother. Out of the corner of his right eye Lane saw a woman studying him. She sat in the aisle seat behind Christine. The woman looked to be in her fifties with short-cut blonde hair. Her eyes were violet and vaguely familiar. Lane began to study her as she leaned forward in her seat. A smile played on her lips. She nodded at him, then turned when the young woman sitting next to her asked a question.

chapter 2

The next time he saw her was at the resort. She wore a white one-piece bathing suit and was slick with sunscreen on pale Canadian skin. The wind was combing its fingers through the fronds of the palm trees near the pool. Arthur wore a white cotton shirt covering his round belly. A white straw panama hat, black shorts and sandals finished the look. Lane saw the woman reading a book. There was cursing. Arthur tripped and fell to his knees, then on his face. His hat rolled along the concrete walkway. Lane stopped. "Arthur?"

Arthur rolled on his back and sat up. He put his hand to his lip. The tip of his finger came away bloody.

Lane put his hand on Arthur's shoulder.

"Did I break my tooth?" Arthur lifted his top lip.

Lane looked at the upper row of front teeth. He pointed at Arthur's bottom lip. "Your teeth are okay. It's just your lip." He reached down, grabbed Arthur's hand and pulled him to his feet.

"He okay?"

They looked left. The woman in the white bathing suit had wrapped a blue skirt around her hips and stood before them.

Arthur said, "Cut my lip and scraped my hand. Damned clumsy." He held out his palm to reveal a red patch.

The woman took his hand, then looked at his lip. She turned and asked, "How have you been, Paul?"

Lane focused on the woman's violet eyes. "I'm usually very good at remembering faces."

She held out her hand. "Gloria. It's been more than thirty years."

He turned his head to the right and studied her with his left eye.

"I was your neighbour. Sometimes I would babysit. Until..." Her eyes dropped and she looked at the red nail polish on her toes.

"You okay?" The voice was male and came from the other side of the pool.

Lane looked over and saw a portly male striding toward them. He had far more hair on his chest, face and arms than remained on his head.

"Do you have some antibiotic cream?" Gloria looked at Arthur, who nodded.

"You'll probably have a bruise. Clean the scrapes and put the cream on them. They'll heal better." Gloria turned and walked back to the pool.

Arthur turned to Lane. "You know her?"

"Apparently." Gloria was gone.

"We'd better get back to the room and get ready for supper. Lola arrived this afternoon. We have dinner reservations. Christine is nervous and wants us to be there." Arthur touched his mouth. "And I need to put some ice on this or my lip will be the size of a beach ball."

×

Three sides of the restaurant were surrounded by water. They could see the fountain at the centre of the pool outside the restaurant window. Lola sat at the head of one end of the table. She wore a cream-coloured pantsuit with an open collar framing generous cleavage and a diamond necklace on a white-gold chain. Lane and Arthur wore shorts, white shirts and sandals. They sat across from the window next to Matt. Christine arrived wearing a white blouse and yellow linen slacks. Dan followed with Indiana on his hip. They wore matching black T-shirts and pants.

Lola frowned and looked at her husband, who had on a grey jacket and tie despite the heat. She pointed at her son. "I hope that you're not wearing that to the wedding. You were raised to be classier than that." Lola looked at Christine and rolled her eyes.

The tone of the comment was a slap stopping Christine within arm's reach of the chair at the other end of the table. She turned, took Indiana from Dan and walked out of the restaurant. Dan shook his head, took a long slow breath, glared at his mother, then followed Christine.

Matt stood up and looked at his uncles. "Wanna go to the buffet? They have great desserts!" He followed Dan.

"What did I say?" Lola's tone had changed from aggressor to victim. She looked expectantly at her husband.

"It's the way you said it. Christine doesn't like anyone talking down to her family." Arthur stood, tucking his chair in.

Lola looked up at Arthur, her eyes hard with anger. Arthur crossed his arms and stood waiting as if to say *Bring it*.

Lola said, "That girl is too sensitive."

Lane felt his anger boil. He moved forward. Arthur put his arm out, startling Lane as he shook his head side to side. "I can handle this."

Dan's father said, "When a new person, an outsider, becomes part of a family, it can break apart."

Lola nodded.

Lane opened his mouth. Arthur held up his hand, then said, "Daniel has joined our family. He is an insider. Now Indiana is part of the family as well. You may wish to continue to blame Christine for your problems and perhaps see Indiana infrequently. Or you could look at your faces in the mirror and fix this." He turned and used the flat of his hand against Lane's chest. "Let's go."

Outside of the restaurant where a cooling breeze blew, Matt said, "Come on, you two, we're going to the buffet.

You know what Christine is like. We need to show her we are behind her and Dan and Indiana. Her mom has also been laying a guilt trip on her for getting married in Cuba and not at the temple, so she needs us."

"What kind of guilt trip?" Lane asked as he rushed to catch up to Matt, who was making good time despite his herky-jerky, skip-hop walk.

"She told me not to say anything." Matt threw the comment over his shoulder as they travelled the palm tree-lined concrete pathway to the buffet restaurant. He waited and held the door for them to enter the wide-open room where tables surrounded the round raised counters loaded with fresh fruit and vegetables, fish and sausage and cheese, hot plates and fresh shrimp, and a wide variety of desserts, including a chocolate fountain. They found Christine sitting near a window, staring off into the deepening tropical night. Indiana sat on her lap and stuffed his fingers into his mouth. Matt tapped Christine on the shoulder. "Okay if we join you?"

She turned, saw the three of them and shrugged. Matt moved some chairs and, aided by Lane and Arthur, pulled over a second table.

Daniel arrived with two plates of food and set one in front of Indiana and the other in front of the empty chair. He reached for Indiana and said to Christine, "You need to get something." She shook her head. Arthur put his hand on her shoulder, and she said, "Go get something to eat. I'll eat in a few minutes. I'm too upset right now." Matt and his uncle left for the buffet.

The waitress arrived. "Wine? *Agua?*"

Lane held up his water glass. "Please." As she poured the water, he watched his niece. "Have some water."

"Don't tell me what to do. I'm sick of people telling me what to do. What my son should wear. Where I should get married. How I should live my life. All the mistakes I've made." She turned her eyes on Lane. It was like being flashed by over-bright headlights on a lonely stretch of prairie highway at midnight. "How come some people think it's okay to treat me like that?"

Lane raised his glass and sipped.

"When I went to see my mother and told her I was coming here get married, she said it wouldn't be sanctified by God unless it happened in the temple. She said Indiana had to be baptized in the temple or he would be barred from heaven. She said I was a criminal for not following God's rules. Now I'm being told my son is not dressed well enough to suit Lola. And it's implied I'm no good for Dan."

"I want to ask a question." Daniel held Indiana with one hand while the baby drank from a bottle of formula.

"Lola told me I should be breast-feeding him. That it was bad for his immune system that I decided to switch to formula." Christine wiped at the condensation on her water glass.

"I would like to change my last name to Lane." Daniel spotted a ring of calamari on his plate, picked it up and popped it in his mouth.

Lane turned to Daniel, realized he'd left his mouth open and closed it.

"What are you talking about?" Christine stared at her fiancé.

Dan picked up anther morsel of calamari and pointed it at Christine and Lane. "I'm asking you two if you would mind if I legally changed my last name to yours." The ring of calamari disappeared into his mouth.

Christine turned to look at Lane. *She's as surprised as I am.*

"It makes perfect sense." Dan pointed with another white circle, popped it in his mouth and chewed. "You want Indiana's last name to stay the way it is on the birth certificate. I'm his father and we're a family." He made a circle with his free hand and grabbed another morsel of calamari. "I want to have the same name as my family."

"What will your mom and dad say?" Christine asked.

"I'm not asking them. I'm asking you. That outsider comment really pissed me off."

Indiana used two hands to lift his bottle over his head and spike it onto the floor. It shattered, leaving a swipe of milk embedded with glass.

In a moment their table was surrounded by staff sweeping up bits of glass, mopping up the mess and smiling. The man with the mop looked at Indy and said, "Baseball!"

×

Lane and Arthur went back to their room. They followed a winding pathway lined by coconut trees. A pair of planets hung in the night sky. Arthur asked, "Do you think Christine and Dan will be okay?"

Lane thought, *Why do Christine and Dan have to have such self-absorbed parents?*

"Well?" Arthur tapped Lane on the shoulder.

"I was thinking that neither of them have much luck with their parents. Alison is mentally ill and Lola thinks she has to be in control. She gives them money for the wedding, says no strings attached, then pulls the strings. I don't think she's able to stop herself." He waited while Arthur opened the door to their ground-floor room.

Arthur went inside where the air conditioner took the edge off the heat and humidity. "What do we do?"

"First off, I'm glad we paid our own way here. She's not going to pull our strings. Anyway, Lola isn't going to listen to either of us even though you told her what the problem is. The only person — and this will sound crazy — who is really able to influence her is Indiana."

Arthur took off his shirt and hung it up. His back was furry with black hair that appeared to have migrated from the top of his head. "This holiday could turn out to be a disaster."

"Too soon to tell, really. Besides, it's a holiday. What's to stop us from having a good time?"

×

Lane slept in his childhood bed. The window was open and the curtains billowed into the room, then were sucked back against the window screen. He could feel the house breathing.

The neighbours' back-door hinges complained when the screen door opened. It rattled when it slapped back against its frame.

He flipped back the covers and put his feet on the hardwood floor. In one part of his mind he wondered why he had an adult body and why he'd woken in a room he hadn't visited for more than thirty years. In this new reality it all seemed completely natural. He went to the window where the curtains billowed. His fingertips separated the drapes. The light over the neighbours' back door reflected off Gloria's white cotton shirt and pants. She held a shovel in her right hand. She went to the nearest corner of the yard. Lane saw her stab the shovel into the earth and push the blade deeper with her right foot. He heard the metal carve into the earth. Gloria inhaled then exhaled. A shovelful of soil was dumped on grass. The process repeated itself again and again.

A different sound. High pitched. Crying. It was joined by Gloria's weeping. He saw her lift a baby from the hole. She moved to the side of the house. He heard the rush of running water from a garden hose. A sharp intake of breath; the infant cried louder. Gloria took off her white cotton blouse and wiped the baby clean and dry, then wrapped the child, holding it close and making soothing sounds.

Then a shock, the slap of the back of a hand across Lane's neck. He felt the cry stuck in his throat, that familiar childhood fear of being under dark attack from his mother.

"What do think you are doing?" His mother's voice was shrill. Then the sting of a belt across his back. Lane turned to grab the leather as it slashed his palm. He yanked it from her hands. The look of anger, then fear, in her eyes as he raised the belt in his fist and moved closer.

Lane sensed a hand on his shoulder. He shrugged it away. A pillow slapped his face. He opened his eyes.

Lights were on in the room. Arthur stood between the queen-sized beds. He was naked, holding a pillow over his right shoulder, ready to strike from a distance.

Lane looked down at his heaving, glistening chest.

Arthur said, "First you screamed, then you roared. I couldn't understand the words. Was it Dr. Pierce again or Cori or both of them?" Arthur dropped the pillow on the bed and began a search for his shorts.

Lane shook his head. "It was a dream from my childhood. That woman from the pool, she was in it."

"Gloria?"

Lane took a long heaving breath. "It was her. She lived next door. I remember her now." He got up to get a bottle of water from the fridge.

"Tell me."

chapter 3

Lane and Arthur sat next to each other on the air-conditioned charter bus. Both looked out the window at the stone walls of the fort standing guard over the Havana Harbour.

Angella was their tour guide and stood next to the driver while speaking into a microphone. "We will soon be arriving at Old Havana, where you will be able to get out, stretch your legs and see a statue of Mother Teresa." Angella wore a red golf shirt, jeans and a white ball cap. Her skin was the colour of the cream atop a *solo café* (what the waitress had called black coffee earlier that morning at the resort restaurant). She kept her long black hair tied in a ponytail, tucked out the back of a Blue Jays ball cap. Lane often had to listen carefully to understand Angella's exotic Cuban English pronunciations.

The stone walls of a church rose up on the right side. The driver slowed, pulled to the right and stopped. People began to stand and stretch after the two-hour ride.

A camera flashed. A woman lined up behind Lane said, "Jamey! Just wait. There will be lots of time for pictures when we get off."

"I wonder how much it costs to go to the bathroom here?" A woman with a clip at the back of her chestnut hair stood up front of them.

"We'll meet in the square in front of the church." Angella waved and stepped off the bus.

Lane and Arthur gathered with the other passengers around the tour guide. Arthur said, "Everywhere she goes, a crowd of people with cameras follows."

Lane smiled as he looked up at the towering grey wall. Arthur nudged Lane's right arm with the water bottle. Lane took the blue glass bottle and raised it to his lips.

"Don't drink too much. It'll cost you later in the bathroom. They charge extra for toilet paper!" The woman with the chestnut hair rubbed her thumb and two adjoining fingers together.

She's quite attractive. Every time she opens her mouth she becomes a little less so. Lane shook his head, sighed and took a long pull on the bottle, then looked away.

Arthur nudged him in the ribs. "Be nice."

Lane rolled his eyes. Jamey stepped in front of Lane. The boy appeared to be ten or eleven, had thick black hair, weighed perhaps eighty pounds and darted in and out with his SLR camera and its black telephoto lens.

"Behave yourself. We have to spend the rest of the day with these people," Arthur said, then turned and followed as they headed for the statue of Mother Teresa. They found her in an alcove in front of a chained-off doorway to a church under renovation. To the left was a lush garden; behind their backs, a steady stream of traffic. Angella tried to make herself heard over the noise. Instead she inhaled some diesel soot and began to cough. She led them back around the church and down a cobbled street. They passed a hotel with a statue of a monk out front; inside were men dressed in tan robes. A minute later they found themselves in a plaza where pigeons surrounded a toddler who was about to cry. His father kept his hands at the boy's back, encouraging him to feed the birds.

Since she was tall enough to be seen over the heads of those gathered around, Angella began to speak. "We will walk down Agaur and then stop at a bar where Hemingway did some of his writing. The bar makes the best mojitos in the city."

"Yes, but does it have a bathroom?" Chestnut Hair adjusted her hair clip until the lines in the corners of her eyes disappeared. "And how much will it cost?" She looked around for support. "Anyone else from Calgary?"

Sometimes it's embarrassing to be Canadian, Lane thought.

The tour guide either did not hear or chose to ignore Chestnut Hair and walked toward a cobblestone street. It ran in between three- and four-storey buildings with metre-wide sidewalks. A black Buick sat at the corner of an intersection. Across the street a pair of female police officers wore grey uniform shirts and black slacks, along with batons and riot sticks on one hip and handguns on the other.

As the group neared another square, music and song echoed along the street from a courtyard. Malabaristas in red, white and black costumes balanced on stilts as they danced and sang. They appeared to walk on the heads of the crowd blocking the street.

Jamey held his camera high, dodging ahead of the tour guide and squeezing between two of the taller people in the crowd. He disappeared as he worked his way to the front where he could get some pictures.

Angella angled to the left side of the crowd and slipped into the open front doors of a bar. Lane followed Arthur as he eased around the crowd and followed Chestnut Hair. She trailed her black-ball-capped husband into the bar where large framed photos of Hemingway hung on the walls and an enlarged copy of his signature hung beneath the collection of black-and-white images.

Arthur asked, "Do you want a mojito?"

Lane nodded and went to inspect the photographs while the bartender lined up ten glasses along his edge of the bar and began by adding mint to the mojitos.

Black Cap came out of the washroom. "Man, that water was cold!"

His friend with the thick dark hair laughed. "Don't let it hang so low, man!"

Chestnut Hair laughed and punched Dark Hair in the shoulder.

Arthur handed Lane a mojito. He sipped the mixture of mint, rum and lime. It was a potent combination on the tongue and in the nose. For a moment he was frozen by the sensation.

After they finished their drinks, they went outside to watch the malabaristas finish performing. A cop dressed in blue with a beret, a goatee and a pistol on his hip made a revolutionary salute, then stood with his hands on his hips. Black Cap took a picture. The cop held up one finger, "Peso."

Black Cap looked at the pistol on the cop/street performer's hip and handed over a peso.

Chestnut Hair pointed at her husband. "Pussy!"

Black Cap turned on her. Lane saw rage behind his eyes. *Watch that one!*

Arthur grabbed Lane's arm and pointed. Three small dogs sat in a cart. They wore vests and revolutionary berets. Dark Hair took a picture and the bald man who owned the dogs said, "Peso." Dark Hair glanced at Chestnut Hair, then said, "No!"

Chestnut Hair threw back her head, winked and laughed.

The man with the dogs frowned, then turned and posed for the next customer.

Arthur took Lane's arm and they followed Angella down another street where she stopped in front of a sculpted face set in a yellow wall of squares. BVZON was written above the stone face, its open mouth set in a pout. The tour guide said, "This is where people deposited letters."

"Did it cost a peso?" Chestnut Hair asked.

Dark Hair smiled at her, then said, "They ripped off the tourists even back in the day."

An unmuffled engine powered an orange bucket set atop four wheels. The driver sat at the back next to the engine. It puffed black sooty smoke. The street filled with the pounding clatter. The tourists moved to the sidewalks on either side of the street to allow the machine to pass. A tall woman in a white dress walked against the foot traffic. She was twenty-five and willowy, moved like a dancer and looked like she modelled for *Vogue*. Every head, including that of the driver of the miniature dump truck, turned to watch as she passed. Jamey stopped in front of Lane, turned and raised his camera. Lane heard the *click, click, click* of multiple exposures. A cloud of exhaust remained. The stink of burned and unburned gasoline made Lane cough. The machine turned left at an intersection; then Angella led them back to the bus.

Lane and Arthur climbed on board. Angella did a head count, frowned and counted again. She went up front and looked at her list, then counted again. "We're missing someone." Lane looked at the empty seat in front of him. Chestnut Hair wasn't sitting next to Black Cap.

Where did she get to? Lane waited for Black Cap to say something, but the man remained silent as he watched the women standing outside with their sleeping infants. The women used their eyes and a free hand to plead for spare change. Arthur elbowed Lane and handed him five pesos. Lane got up, walked to the front of the bus and handed the pesos to one of the women. All at once, two boys, two women and an old man with one good eye surrounded him. He moved back to the door as one of the boys clutched at his shirt and asked, "What about us?" The driver shut the door when Lane made it back inside.

The driver shook his head and pointed at the boys, who had moved on to another tourist who had given a coin to the old man. The driver said, "I know those boys. Their parents live in one of the city's most beautiful houses."

×

They arrived at the returning tour's first stop at seven that evening. Two women in grey long-sleeved shirts and black pants were waiting with their arms crossed, their long hair gathered on top of their heads. Each wore a pistol on one hip and a riot stick on the other. A pair of Russian-built trucks in military green pulled up behind the tour bus. Another approached the wrong way up the road and parked out front of the bus.

Angella stepped off the bus and began to talk with the officers. Then the tour guide climbed back on the bus. "The police say that all of us are to follow them to the resort's meeting room. Please have your identification ready."

A woman at the back of the bus said, "I was told I didn't need my ID."

"The police say we must come with them and identify ourselves," Angella said.

Lane stood up. "The faster we answer the questions, the sooner we'll get back to our own hotels." He made his way to the front of the bus and stepped down out onto the paved driveway. Arthur followed him, and then other passengers reluctantly got off the bus as well.

The police officers studied Lane as he walked toward them. One had her hands on her hips. The other crossed her arms under her breasts. She leaned her head to the right toward an officer who stood in the empty foyer of the resort. He was flanked by flowerpots filled with birds of paradise. He motioned Lane forward. Gradually, the other passengers gathered in a room with tables surrounded by upholstered chairs. Lane sat near the far wall and turned to Arthur, who sat next to him. "Let's just watch."

Arthur shook his head. "Don't you dare enjoy this."

"The missing woman must be dead or badly injured for them to make this much of a fuss." Lane took a slow breath and waited.

It was Arthur's turn to be interviewed an hour later.

Lane watched his partner disappear into an adjoining room. The massive wooden doors closed. The words *Night Club* were written in wrought iron above the doors. He turned to watch the people who remained. Black Cap sat sipping a piña colada and avoiding eye contact with any of the others. Dark Hair looked about nervously as he leaned against the wall opposite the husband of the missing woman. He used a paper napkin to wipe away the sweat from his face. The front of his pale-blue shirt was stained darker by a sweaty patch.

Jamey looked at the back of his digital camera and scrolled through the images.

Angella watched the comings and goings as individuals were escorted to and from the bathroom. A woman arrived with a tray of sandwiches. Two servers manoeuvred their way around the tables as they took and delivered drink orders. Angella talked to the bald-headed driver, who shook his head and shrugged in the universal expression of an individual's loss of control over a situation.

The massive wooden doors opened, the larger police-woman appeared and said in accented English, "Paul Lane!"

Lane stood, stepped into the nightclub and saw a single table in the middle of the room. One female officer sat there and watched his arrival. Her eyes were black, her skin was tan and her black hair shone under the lights. He estimated she might be thirty. She said, "Sit down. *Por favor.*"

He did as instructed, sat across the table from her and decided the solidly built officer across from him was nobody's fool. The other officer sat down, took a pen in her hand, flipped over a fresh piece of paper on her notepad and waited. Her name tag identified her as Adelsie Romirez.

"Citizenship?" the officer in charge asked.

"Canadian. Your name, *por favor*?" Lane watched the other woman scribble her notes.

"Deylis Sanchez. A woman is missing. What is your occupation?"

Lane said, "Homicide detective with the Calgary Police Service."

The other officer stopped writing and looked at Deylis, who studied Lane for at least thirty seconds. "What can you tell us about the missing woman?"

"The woman with the chestnut hair who sat in front of us on the bus? She was about thirty-five. She wore a red dress and her hair was held at the back with a clip." He mimed placing a spring-loaded clip at the back of his head.

"Clip?" Deylis looked puzzled.

"A plastic clip with teeth to hold her hair at the back." He mimed again.

Deylis nodded and waited.

Lane did the same. *Don't piss her off. Wait for her lead. You're in Cuba. You don't know the rules here. Besides, you're on her turf.*

"You did notice her then?"

Lane nodded. "She sat in front of me on the bus and complained."

"What did she complain about?" Deylis crossed one leg over the other, leaned back and studied him again.

"Having to tip the attendant at the washroom where we stopped about midway between Havana and Varadero. The food, the heat, the road, the socialist government of Cuba..."

"You did not like this woman?" Deylis leaned forward.

You walked right into that one. "No, I did not. She was rude, loud, arrogant and she treated other people—especially Cubans—with contempt."

"She was from the same city as you."

"That is correct." Lane waited.

"Did you know her from before?"

Lane shook his head.

Deylis glanced at the door. "What did you notice about her husband?"

"The man in the black ball cap?"

"Yes." Deylis glanced at Adelsie, who continued to write without lifting her head.

"When the tour guide asked who was missing, he remained silent. His wife treated him with disrespect from the beginning of the tour until the end."

"What do you mean by the end?"

"The last time I remember seeing her was when the construction machine passed us."

Deylis leaned forward. "Describe this machine."

"It was like a small dump truck with four wheels and a driver at the back."

Deylis nodded. "Anything else?"

"They were angry with one another."

"About what?"

Lane shook his head. "I'm not sure. All I know is that there was tension between them."

Deylis nodded and looked at the door. Her phone rang. She took it from the pouch on her belt, looked at the number, pressed a button and held the phone to her ear. There were rapid words in Spanish. Lane saw Adelsie raise her head. Deylis said, "*Gracias*," then pressed a button and replaced the phone in its holster.

Lane waited for Deylis.

"Which hotel are you staying at?" Deylis stood up.

"Iberostar. Playa Alemeda."

"Room number?"

"One four one nine."

Deylis reached into her breast pocket and handed Lane a card. "If you think of anything else, I would like you to call this number and ask for me." She pointed at him. "I want the phone number and name of your superior to verify your identity."

Lane gave her the name and number, took the card and nodded.

"You may go." She pointed at a door to the right. As Lane opened the door she said, "You and all of the other passengers may not be allowed to leave Cuba until this situation is resolved. You will be asked to relinquish your passports."

Lane turned to say something, thought better of it and left.

×

Matt and Christine were waiting in the Iberostar's octagonal lobby with its eight pillars when the tour bus dropped Lane, Arthur, Jamey and his parents off.

"It's three in the morning. Where have you been?" Christine got up from the red couch and walked toward them.

Lane smiled.

Matt caught up to his cousin. "What's so funny? No one would tell us where you were."

"The staff won't say a word. It's like they've all been told to keep quiet," Christine said.

"Where are Indy and Dan?" Arthur asked.

"Asleep." Christine tucked her arm inside Lane's elbow. "Do you know what's going on?"

"A woman on our tour went missing." He began to walk toward the back of the lobby. "We need to get some sleep."

"Did they find her?" Matt asked.

"Is she okay?" Christine asked.

"She's dead," Arthur said.

Lane looked at Arthur, who winked and shrugged. "Doesn't take a detective to figure out that they wouldn't go to all of this trouble over a person who was missing for less than twelve hours."

chapter 4

Lane walked the relatively solid sand. He tried to follow the constantly shifting edge where the ocean and beach met and the sand was firm under the feet. When he looked left, the ocean went from light green to more emerald deep-water shades. On the beach, people sunbathed and drank rum in a variety of flavoured combinations. A few smoked cigars. Lane caught a whiff of smoke. It carried a memory: his father smoking in the car in winter despite the chorus of complaints from his children in the back seat.

Lane wore a white shirt and black shorts. He carried his sandals in his right hand. Out in the ocean, wind riders cut the waves on solo boards as they manoeuvred their kites in the stiff wind, transforming them into hybrid creatures. Equal parts wind, water and flesh skipping, carving and flying the waves.

He walked and deliberated. Christine's wedding, the disappearance of the woman from the bus and the man he had killed all washed in and out of his consciousness. The waves ran up his calves as he tried to make sense of the undercurrents of thoughts swimming at and under the surface.

Christine wants Arthur and me to walk her down the aisle. Indiana will be the ring bearer. Matt is Daniel's best man. Lola wants to control the event and is driving the staff crazy as she nitpicks over the details. Having Daniel change his last name will certainly cause some kind of negative reaction from Lola. I wonder how her husband John became so whipped?

Then a flashback of shooting Professor Pierce.

The woman with the chestnut hair is almost certainly dead. I'm sure that's what Deylis was told over the phone last night. Right now it looks like the husband killed her. The look on his face. What she said to him. The man with the black hair she was flirting with. A beautiful and unfaithful woman. A jealous husband. Such a cliché. And so often a recipe for violence.

Another flashback of a one-eyed Dr. Pierce hit like a wave. The muzzle flash from the professor's weapon. The recoil of Lane's Glock. The smell of burnt gun oil. The rasp of Pierce's breathing. The empty look in his remaining eye as his blood drained out at the feet of the boy he had been about to kill.

Lane felt the wind tugging at his clothing. The taste of the sea on his tongue. A wave ran frothy white up the beach and splashed up his ankles. *Walking usually brings some clarity.* A hand touched his shoulder. Lane turned and saw anguish on Daniel's face. "What's happened?"

"Christine went to talk with my mother and work things out. They argued. My mother wants the money back for the wedding."

"Walk with me." Lane took Dan's elbow and they walked into the wind. Lane waited until they found a rhythm and after that some clarity of thought.

"What do I do?" Daniel stumbled as a wave rolled far up the beach and pushed at their knees.

"First you let everyone cool down. You and Christine go to Varadero or the Dolphinario. Take Matt with you if you like." He reached into his shirt pocket and handed Dan four twenties. "Arthur and I will watch Indiana. Wait for your mother to come to you. The wedding is two days from now. Lola organized it." He looked sideways at Daniel, gauging how much more or little to say.

"And?"

"She will want to see it happen."

"What about paying for it? My mother is known for being ruthless with money. Especially when she doesn't get what she wants."

"First off, I'm pretty sure the entire event is prepaid. So it may be an empty threat." Lane reached into his other shirt pocket and pulled out a gold plastic card. "If not, this is exactly the kind of situation credit cards are for."

Daniel shook his head. "Christine said you would be calm and you'd have a plan."

Lane smiled. *This is not life or death. This is a problem that can be fixed.* "If you and I can keep our cool, things will have a better chance of working themselves out."

Daniel turned to go back. Lane took him by the arm. "Let's walk a bit further. Christine needs some time to cool off. You and I need to walk a bit longer to clear our minds."

They walked fifty metres. A man in a navy-blue Speedo approached. He was over six feet tall with broad shoulders and the beginnings of a tan. As he got closer, they could see that his bathing suit was so low cut in the front that pubic hairs curled out and over the front. He passed.

Dan looked at Lane.

I wonder what he'll say, Lane thought.

Twenty metres later, Dan asked, "I gotta know. Is that why women first painted on the walls of caves?"

Lane smiled. "Just wait. When you think you've seen something really strange, something at least as weird will happen on the beach."

After walking for at least half a kilometre, they turned and headed back to the resort. They walked up through a gap in the trees, along a wooden sidewalk and onto a concrete pathway leading to a white column. It had running water and they washed their feet. Dan tapped Lane on the shoulder and pointed. "What's that?"

Lane turned and saw three side-by-side green concrete portals. The structure sat about half a metre above ground. "I'm not sure."

They walked toward their building. As they approached they saw another flat-topped concrete structure with portals like the last. Lane said, "I think it's a machine gun emplacement." He pointed. "It's aimed at the beach. A waterborne invasion force would be greeted by machine-gun fire."

Dan frowned and looked up at the second-floor balcony where Christine and Indiana waited. "Weird. Our wedding ceremony will take place by a concrete gun emplacement." He pointed at the wooden platform where the event was scheduled to take place. "Kind of apropos, wouldn't you say?"

Lane nodded and smiled. "You've got your perspective back."

×

Arthur and Indiana napped. Lane listened to Norah Jones on his iPad and sat outside on the patio as he tried to read *Prodigal Summer* by Barbara Kingsolver. He looked up from the novel and watched as the wind blew at the tops of the coconut trees.

A woman in dark slacks and grey shirt walked on the sidewalk on the other side of the bougainvilleas in front of his room. Lane sat up.

Deylis Sanchez appeared around this side of the bougainvilleas. "Mr. Lane."

Lane removed the headphones, turned off the music and set down his iPad. "Detective." Lane saw a slight smile cross her lips.

"Have you remembered any other details about the missing woman?"

He opened his left hand to tell her she could sit, and she did. "Would you like a coffee?"

"A glass of water?" She crossed her right leg over her left knee.

Lane got up, opened the sliding glass door carefully, went into the fridge and grabbed a bottle of water. Arthur snored while Indy lay flat on his back in the other bed. Lane backed out of the room. He handed the water to Deylis, who nodded. "*Gracias.*" She twisted off the cap and began to drink.

Lane said, "How was she murdered?"

Deylis choked. Lane patted her on the back. She caught her breath and took another sip. "How did you know?"

"You are going to way too much trouble for a person who might have gotten lost and missed the bus."

"A missing tourist would mean a cold for our economy. A murdered tourist could mean pneumonia. Our country is just getting back on its feet again. There is concern about the way this woman died and what it will do to Cuba's reputation as a safe place for tourists." Deylis put the cap on her water bottle, then set it on the coffee table.

"I've been thinking about the case and what I saw and heard. They sat in front of us on the bus all of the way to Havana. The husband and wife were angry with one another. She made him look small in front of another man who was her age and had thick black hair. He was not from this resort. I've been trying to remember where he got on the bus and am having no luck. The last time I saw the husband and wife together was near the face on the wall with the open mouth — the mailbox."

"Buzon," Deylis said.

Lane looked at her with a frown.

"The face with the open mouth for mailing letters. It's called Buzon."

Lane nodded. "It was also at the time when a construction vehicle came down the street."

"The moto volqueta?"

Lane asked, "The noisy orange bucket on four wheels with the driver riding behind?"

"That's correct."

"I've thought about what happened. That was the time and place where I last saw the woman."

"Did you have a camera?"

Lane got up, went inside the room and returned with a small camera. He turned it on and handed it to her.

She scrolled through the pictures. "They are very small." She held up the camera. "Can I take this and return it to you?"

Lane nodded.

"My — how you say?" She thought for a moment, searching for the right word. Her eyes opened and she smiled. "My boss called your boss."

"Simpson?"

"Yes, that is the name. Your boss said that in your city you are a very good hunter for killers. That you would be a good help to this investigation."

Hold on! He looked over his shoulder to see if Arthur was there. "My niece is getting married in two days."

"I know this. I need you to come to Havana with me right now."

"This is my holiday." Lane looked at Deylis's eyes and recognized what he saw. *She's on the hunt. You cannot underestimate this one. She's done her homework and already knows I will go with her.* "I'll have to talk with Arthur first."

"We know this as well. Your boss made my boss give his word that you would be protected. Cuban law is a little . . . ."

Lane waited and felt that hidden anxiety rising up from a place he had almost forgotten.

"Old-fashioned."

Lane waited.

"You have my word and the word of my boss that you and your Arthur, all of your family, will be protected. From this antiquated law and from the killer."

Lane inhaled, dropped his chin and shook his head. "Shit."

"It is a curse you and I must face up to. I see it in your eyes as well. We are hunters. We cannot escape this fact."

Lane lifted his head and smiled. "You're right about it being a curse."

×

"You've got be fucking joking." Arthur's raspy comment kept playing over in Lane's mind. *I should have gone to the bathroom before I left.*

Deylis turned in the front seat of the car to face him. "You are worried about your Arthur?"

Lane nodded. He saw the driver glance at him in the rear-view mirror. *It's pretty clear that Deylis does not trust him. She has said almost nothing in the last two hours.* Lane saw the now-familiar outline of the fort looking down onto Havana Harbour. Deylis turned to the driver, pointed to her right and said something in Spanish. The driver shoulder checked, changed lanes, braked and stopped at the side of the road. Deylis opened her door, got out and opened Lane's door. He squeezed out of the back seat of the tiny four-door Gilly, a car he'd never seen in Canada. *That would have been uncomfortable even when I was ten.* He stood up in the humid heat of the afternoon and inhaled the often-overpowering aromas of the city.

"Hector will wait in the car." Deylis led Lane down a narrow cobblestone street. He hurried to catch up. At this time in the afternoon there were fewer tourists and Lane saw the city more as a resident might see it. Deylis skirted the edge of a courtyard with its yellow, blue and green painted shops and apartments. Lane saw the pigeons had left because the tourists were no longer there. Deylis went down another street. Even the sound of the construction was silenced. A long-legged, white-haired man in tan dress slacks and a tan sports jacket sat in a chair just outside a doorway. His legs stretched out into the street. He nodded as they passed, and puffed on a cigar.

Deylis stopped in front of the open mouth of the gargoyle that no longer accepted letters. She pointed down the street. "This is where you saw the moto volqueta?"

Lane looked at the street and the black 1955 Buick parked at one end. He crossed to the sidewalk where he had been standing. "There was a woman. A beautiful young woman dressed in white. Her skin was about as dark as yours. Every eye in this street was on her as she walked along that sidewalk." He pointed at the sidewalk on the other side of the street. "The moto volqueta was over there. People were forced to either sidewalk so it could pass. It was so loud that it was impossible to hear anything else. The man and his wife were the last in our tour group."

Deylis nodded. "That's very similar to what the driver of the moto volqueta said. He has already been arrested. I don't think he is the killer." She turned and looked back the way they had come.

"I need to find a bathroom."

Deylis frowned.

"*Baño, por favor.*" *I hope that works because it's about all the Spanish I know.*

"Of course." She swung one hundred eighty degrees, leading the way down the street. Lane followed.

They reached an intersection. She looked left, then took a right. Lane followed. *Deylis, for Christ's sake, slow down! This isn't an Olympic event!*

She walked through the swinging chrome doors of a bar. Lane's eyes took a moment to adjust to the darkness.

A couple sat on stools in the corner. They watched both Lane and Deylis with suspicion. Lane saw the washroom door and went inside. He closed the door and stood facing a toilet without a seat. Next to the toilet was a can containing blood-stained sanitary napkins. He leaned over the toilet and when he was done washed his hands. He walked out only to be confronted by the bartender, who was arguing with Deylis. He pointed at Lane and said, "Peso!"

Lane saw Deylis's spine straighten with anger. He touched her shoulder, reached into the pocket of his shorts, pulled out a peso, put it on the bar and led the way out.

"I'm trying to solve a murder and that *pinche pendejo* is worried about his peso! What will happen to his business if the tourists stop coming?" Deylis was walking even faster than before.

"Hey!" Lane stopped in the middle of the street. *I hope I don't get run over. No one stops for pedestrians in this country.*

Deylis turned. Her face was red with anger. "A man has been arrested. I believe he is not guilty. There is limited time."

"I can think more clearly if we can walk a little slower." He held up his thumb and forefinger with about two millimetres in between.

She threw her hands in the air. "Come this way." She walked, stopped, waited for him to catch up, then tucked her left arm inside his right elbow. "We will walk together." She turned down one street, then another. The dome of a cathedral appeared in front of them. It was at least two kilometres away. *I have absolutely no idea where we are.* The streets got grimier, more congested. The stink of diesel and gasoline exhaust intensified. Deylis ducked into a shop, set down a bill, took two newspapers and waited for her change. The shopkeeper was missing one front tooth at the top and another two at the bottom. He handed her five coins, smiled and lisped, "*Gracias, amiga.*"

Deylis went back into the street with the newspapers tucked under her arm. She led them back until they found a park with a stylized cubist mural painted on the side of a building. The colours were red, green, yellow and an intense blue. She sat down on a bench, opened the front of the tabloid and pointed at the headline. "The man who was arrested was driving the moto volqueta. He has four children. He says he is innocent. The woman was discovered unconscious in the bottom of the bucket of his machine. She was taken to the hospital and died after two hours. She had a head injury. The autopsy is not yet complete. The papers are saying this man —" she pointed at the face of the accused "— Omar, is innocent. People are saying that he has been arrested so the government will not be embarrassed. The government is worried about tourism dollars. My boss is getting pressure to solve the case quickly. People are afraid that what happened to tourism in Mexico will happen to Cuba. That the tourists will stop coming and the economy will suffer again. Most people think the tourist killed his wife and that Omar will pay the price."

She pointed at the buildings across the street. One had a fresh coat of yellow paint and stood proud after being restored. Its neighbour was grey and had water stains running down its stone. It was windowless and the cornices at its top were crumbling. Lane could see supporting timbers through the windows. The sun shone through what should have been a roof. "First there was the revolution, then the embargo, then the Soviet Union collapsed. It is our fear that hard economic times will come again and cripple Cuba just when we are getting back on our feet."

Lane tapped her on the shoulder. "Shouldn't we take a look at those photos?"

"Of course!" She slapped her hands on her thighs, stood up and walked down the street. Lane rushed to follow.

An hour later, they sat in front of a computer and looked though the downloaded photos from Arthur's camera. Deylis scrolled through the images until she was able to find the street with the open-mouthed gargoyle. One of Arthur's photos showed the street, the moto volqueta approaching with its orange bucket, the woman in the white clothing walking down the far side. Lane pointed at the screen. "There they are." The husband in the black ball cap stood next to his wife. The moto volqueta was in the middle of the street and the woman was leaning away from it. "What does the next picture show?"

Deylis clicked the mouse. The next image showed the street performers on stilts. They looked toward the camera with their painted faces. She went through the rest of the photos. "I would like to keep copies of these."

Lane nodded, she clicked the mouse and then leaned back to wait. *I'm missing something.*

Deylis said, "I believe the husband lied. He told me that he had no idea what happened to his wife. The driver of the moto volqueta is recognizable in the photo. The husband is recognizable and so is the wife."

"But you will need more evidence to clear the driver."

Deylis nodded. "Yes, I will need more."

"What is the husband's name?"

"Brett Mara."

"And the wife?"

"Camille Mara."

"Both from Calgary?"

"Yes. Calgary, Canada."

×

Lane got out of the passenger seat of the Gilly and waited for the white subcompact to drive out the front gate. Hector had said three words during the two hours it took to drive

Lane back to his hotel. It was a half hour after sunset and he headed for the bar, where he ordered a mojito and waited at a table by himself. He looked at his watch. *I wonder what happened here today?* He took ten minutes to finish the minty drink and watched as other tourists passed by the door. A man with a mustache and green-and-white striped shorts came in, stepped up to the bar and said, "Beer!"

The bartender looked at the man then turned, opened the fridge door and pulled out a can of beer. "Glass?"

"No." The man took the can of beer and left.

Lane studied the bartender and the blank expression on her face. He finished his drink, got up, set the empty glass on the bar and said, "Thank you." The bartender smiled at him. Lane walked outside into the tropical night and headed for his room. When he reached the door, he swiped the lock with his key card and went inside. The bed was made and the room empty. He found a note near the TV. "Gone to supper."

He looked for them at the buffet, saw that swordfish was on the grill and plenty of fresh bread and vegetables were nearby. *I'm starved.* He grabbed a plate, got into line at the grill, then found a table near the window. The peace of the meal went uninterrupted for three minutes.

"You were supposed to meet us for supper!"

Lane looked up as he savoured a morsel of swordfish. Christine stood next to him. Indiana was on her hip with one hand clutching her pink-and-white-striped sleeve. Lane smiled.

"We left you a note."

Adriana the waitress walked up with a pitcher of water. "*Hola*, baby!" She filled Lane's water glass, shook hands with Indy and left.

Lane waited.

"We came here for my wedding. My wedding." Christine pointed at her chest with her free hand. Indiana got his free hand into her black hair and pulled. She disentangled his hand and held it.

"Please sit down." Lane waited while she considered the invitation.

She took a deep breath and sighed. "Okay, explain."

"A woman was killed. The wrong person may be accused. There are political and economic implications." He cut off another piece of swordfish and put it in his mouth, avoiding the temptation to close his eyes and enjoy the gentle flavours of meat, garlic and butter.

"And Cuba doesn't have any police to solve this crime?" Indiana began to squirm; she sat him on her lap. He stuck his fist in his mouth. Drool began to wet the front of his shirt.

Lane shrugged and chewed. *This fish is fabulous.*

"I want my family to be there. I need you to tell me that you will be there."

"I'll be there."

"Promise?"

"Promise."

Indy looked up at his mother, pulled his fist from his mouth and studied the long string of drool running from fingers to gums. Christine stuck her finger in his mouth, "Have you got any teeth yet?"

Indy clamped down on her finger.

"Ouch!" She cringed and pulled her finger out of his mouth. "You!" Then she started to laugh.

chapter 5

Lane and Arthur walked side by side along the beach. The breeze made their shirts flap, and the spray from the ocean tasted salty on the lips.

Two joggers splashed up alongside on the right. Both women wore bikinis. As they passed Lane saw they were both wearing thongs. Their glutes went concave, then convex as they planted and lifted each foot. Lane looked left and saw some male admirers smiling as the two women continued down the beach.

"Are those what are called badonkadonks?" Arthur asked. "Or are they called booties?"

"We're really out of touch. If we ask the kids, they'll probably laugh. When did we get old?"

Lane shrugged. "It must have happened all of a sudden."

Arthur frowned. "I still wonder why we turned out the way we did."

"Why some people find that attractive, yet you and I are simply puzzled because it's kind of grotesque?" Lane shook his head.

"Actually, I was wondering about the little switch in the brain that makes one thing attractive and another distasteful."

A wave ran up the beach and splashed their calves. "At least we can agree that the water is warm."

"Yes, there is that."

A black-haired woman ran to the water. She stood over six feet, weighed close to two hundred pounds, had a muscular physique and wore a neon-pink bikini. Another wave rolled in and ran up to her knees. She squealed. "It's so cold!" She danced back out of the water to reveal pink toenails.

"Or maybe we can't agree about the water." Arthur nodded up the beach. "Your friend is looking for you."

Lane looked and spotted Deylis, who held one hand shading her eyes. She waved with her free hand.

Arthur grabbed Lane's elbow. "The wedding is tomorrow. You will be at Christine's wedding. You will notice that was not a question." He walked up the beach alongside Lane.

When they reached Deylis, Arthur held out his hand. "Arthur."

"Deylis Sanchez. A pleasure." She shook his hand, then pulled him close to kiss his cheek. "Your niece is getting married tomorrow at five. Correct?"

Arthur nodded and looked sideways at Lane. "How did you know?"

"It is my business to know." She leaned her head to one side. "My boss promised his boss that your Lane would be at the wedding. And I am promising you that he will be there."

Arthur smiled. "I will hold both of you to that."

Deylis turned to Lane. "You will come with me to Matanzas?"

×

Deylis sat in the passenger seat again as Hector drove the four-lane highway into Matanzas. They could see across the harbour where tankers docked next to the massive fuel storage tanks. Deylis turned to face Lane and asked, "Did you know that this city is named after a massacre?"

Lane looked at the deeper water in the middle of the harbour. "No, I didn't."

"In the early sixteenth century, the local Indians offered to help Spaniards who were stranded on the far side of the bay. The Indians were aware of the Spaniards' brutality by then, so they loaded about thirty into their canoes, then tipped them over in the middle of the bay where it is very deep." She pointed at the dark green water in the middle. "The men were wearing armour and sank. But two of the women survived." Deylis pointed left and Hector turned.

They arrived in the town square of Matanzas, where pink and fuchsia blossoms adorned the top of a trellis. "Brett Mara left his resort and was spotted here in the city. I want you to listen while I question him. Apparently he is here with another woman. We believe she is Cuban." She pointed at a road leading from the square. "There is an apartment above that building. Will you follow us up the stairs and then join us when we question him? My English is good, but not as good as yours. I need your impressions of the story he tells us." Hector parked the car and they got out. Deylis looked at Lane. "I need to understand his nuances. Is that the right word?"

"It is." Lane nodded as he leaned back and pressed his hands at the base of his spine.

They walked along the street. Lane looked left at a white building with stained glass and the word FRANCESA set in the middle of one pane. A red motorcycle with a sidecar pumped out black smoke as it rattled past. A heavy green Russian truck followed. More black smoke. Lane turned away from the cloud of diesel exhaust. Hector turned right into a doorway and went up a steep set of stairs. Deylis followed him and drew her handgun. Lane followed as they topped the stairs and went down a hallway. Hector had his gun in his right hand and pounded the door with his left. "*Policia!*"

They were greeted by silence. Hector tried three more times. He waited while Deylis knocked on a door across the hallway. A white-haired woman answered and a conversation in Spanish followed. The old woman closed her door.

Deylis looked at Lane. "They left early this morning." She walked down the hallway and knocked on another door. A one-legged man on crutches gave her a key, and she handed it to Hector, who opened the door. The room had no curtains on the windows. The double bed was unmade and the wardrobe door hung open to reveal it was empty.

Lane went down the hall, down the stairs, back out onto the street, and headed for the square where he sat on a bench and waited. *There is something I need to remember.* He watched a tour bus arrive and about fifteen people came out of the building with the stained-glass windows. They followed a tour guide with long dark hair tied in a ponytail. She wore a white blouse and blue pants. She crossed the street with her gaggle behind. As they reached the sidewalk next to the park, a man with a camera bag, a yellow T-shirt and khaki shorts tapped the woman on the shoulder. "Oda?"

She turned and waited for the last of her tour to step on the sidewalk, then said, "Yes."

"You said something about Dr. Triolet's first wife? I missed it. She died unexpectedly when she was twenty and he was over fifty. He said she died of pneumonia, but you said that she didn't. Two months later, he married her sister."

Oda looked at the man who was a foot taller and twice her weight.

"Are you saying he killed her?"

She lowered her chin and lifted her eyebrows. "What do you think?"

Lane saw the man holding his camera and its long lens. Lane's eyes opened wide. "Shit." He turned to his right and saw Deylis walking toward him. She looked disappointed. He waved at her. "Come on!"

Deylis held her hands out as she crossed the street and gave him a quizzical look.

"Hurry!" Lane walked toward the car.

"Did you see Mara?"

He reached for the back door of the car. "No! I just remembered a kid and a camera." He climbed in the back seat.

Deylis opened her door. "I don't understand."

"There was a kid on the Havana tour. He had a telephoto lens and he was shooting pictures nonstop. He's staying at my resort. We need to look at his pictures." Lane reached for his seat belt. "Let's go! Get on your phone and tell them we need to talk with a ten-year-old boy. He's from Toronto. His name is Jamey." *I hope he hasn't left.*

×

It took three calls and twenty minutes before Deylis was able to track down Jamey from Toronto. "He and his family took a tour to the Dolphinario and they leave tomorrow. We are close to where they are supposed to be." She said a few words in Spanish to Hector. Lane understood only one.

It took ten more minutes to arrive at the Dolphinario. Then there was an argument at the ticket wicket. Lane gathered that the woman behind the window thought Lane should pay before they were allowed inside. He pulled out fifteen pesos. The dispute ended. Lane followed Deylis past the souvenir shops and toward the stands set up on one side of an inlet. On the far side, dense foliage reached to the water's edge. Music blared from an ancient, overworked sound system. A pair of dolphins raced across the hundred-metre-wide enclosure. Their speed made the crowd gasp. Deylis took a right, went down the back of the stands and headed for the far end. Lane saw a pair of men exchanging money. They ducked around the end of a small building when one spotted her uniform.

Deylis stopped at the end of the stands and waved Lane ahead. He walked down a narrow concrete sidewalk with the stands on his left and mangroves on his right.

Stepping carefully, Lane walked up to the front where a fence and Plexiglas marked the edge of the lake. A pair of dolphins pushed one of the trainers into the corner where mangroves, dock and fence met. The resultant wave washed up over Lane's shoes. He didn't notice. Instead he looked at the crowd and spotted Jamey almost immediately. The boy held his left eye to the viewfinder of his camera in anticipation of the dolphins' next move.

Lane felt Deylis at his elbow. He said, "Jamey is right here. Now's not the time to interrupt. Let him finish with his pictures. Then we will talk with him."

Deylis frowned.

"Do you know where Mara is?"

She shook her head.

"Jamey will talk after the show is finished. Not before. The kid is really into photography. If we interrupt, we'll get attitude. It will take a little time to save us time."

Deylis raised her eyebrows. Lane waited. Two dolphins launched the trainer into the air. She did a somersault, then jackknifed into the water. One dolphin offered its fin and towed the waving trainer back to the dock. Lane watched dark-haired Jamey, who smiled when he caught a pair of dolphins in mid-air as they flew through two hoops. The detective smiled seeing Jamey held down the shutter so the camera could take multiple frames.

After the show, the detectives waited for the crowd to thin. Jamey sat scrolling through his photos. His father stood up. Lane touched the man's elbow; he looked like a taller, balder version of his dark-haired son.

Deylis asked, "Mr. Colin Anderson, could we talk with your son, Jamey?"

The father frowned. Concern sharpened the focus of his brown eyes when he recognized Deylis's uniform. He looked to see where his son was. "How do you know my name?"

Lane kept his tone even and low. "We were hoping to ask Jamey if we could look at his pictures."

"My son has done nothing wrong." Anderson's response hung somewhere between a statement and a question. He stared at Lane. "Where are you from?"

"Calgary. You're from Toronto?" Lane glanced at Deylis, who watched Jamey.

"You know a lot about me and my son."

Just level with him. He will respect that. "We were hoping that Jamey's camera might hold the answer to a question. It's about what happened on the Havana tour. You and your son are not suspects, but his pictures may hold some answers for us."

"You work down here?" Anderson asked.

"I'm here for my niece's wedding."

Anderson shook his head. "So do you work down here or not?"

Lane shrugged. "Yes." *And no.*

"Jamey, will you talk to the police?"

Jamey was focused on scrolling through his pictures. His father touched his son on the shoulder. Jamey looked up in surprise. "You gotta see this shot, Dad."

"The police are asking if they can look at your pictures."

Jamey held his camera close to his chest.

Lane said. "We just want to look." He glanced at Deylis. "We might ask you to download a photo or two if we find what we're looking for. That's all."

Jamey looked at his father, who shrugged as if to say *Okay with me if it's okay with you.*

"There are some tables around back. We could sit there while you show us the pictures from Havana," Lane suggested.

"Sure." Jamey followed Deylis as she led the way to a table under an umbrella.

Jamey sat down with Lane and Deylis on either side. The boy began to scroll through the images on the screen at the back of his camera.

"Do you know what a moto volqueta is?" Lane asked.

Jamey looked at Lane and smiled. "You mean that little dump truck that made so much noise?"

"That's the one."

Jamey stared intently at the screen, stopped at a series of images, leaned over to show the camera to Lane, then said, "Just press this button."

Lane looked carefully at the images of the moto volqueta, the woman in white, the street; then he stopped. "Is it possible to magnify this one?"

"Sure," Jamey said in a way only a young person with intimate knowledge of technology could while barely masking his disdain for the ignorance of his elders. He pressed a button. Lane moved the image around until he could see a hand and a woman's shoulder. He looked at Deylis. "You need to see this."

"What do you see?" Deylis leaned close to see what Lane was pointing at.

×

Deylis got a call just before reaching the traffic circle out front of Playa Alameda Resort. "Si?"

Lane saw her sit up straighter in her seat. "Matanzas." She pressed end then pointed for Hector to park.

She waited until they stopped. Lane got out and she asked, "Could we get a cup of coffee?"

"Vivian makes a great cappuccino over here." He pointed to the right of the lobby and led the way. They sat down at a table with a round granite top and cast-iron frame.

"What about Hector? Does he want a coffee?" Lane held out a chair for her.

Deylis smiled. "You don't need to worry about Hector. He will find someone to amuse himself."

"Casanova?"

She nodded.

Vivian arrived in her blue and yellow uniform. She smiled. "Cappuccino?"

"Please." Lane smiled, held up two fingers, then reached into his pocket and pulled out a peso.

"I should be putting the money down." Deylis reached into her pocket.

Lane shook his head. "Not on your salary."

Deylis smiled. "That is why Cubans like Canadians. You understand." She frowned, then continued. "The body of Robert North was discovered in Matanzas. It appears he died two days ago."

"Camille Mara's friend?"

Deylis looked at him closely before she nodded.

"Cause of death?"

"It will take an autopsy to confirm, but he was beaten first."

The coffees arrived. Lane stirred in a packet of sugar. "Is there any connection to Brett Mara?"

"They were seen together the night before North's body was discovered. They were drinking at a bar. They left after midnight. North wasn't seen alive after that." She sipped her coffee.

"Any idea where Mara is now?"

"I have an educated guess."

Lane sipped his coffee and waited.

"In the waters between Florida and Cuba it is easy for two ships to find each other and trade cargo. There is a black market in Cuba. I think Mara found someone in Matanzas who would take him to a ship bound for the US in exchange for money."

"Do your navy and the American navy patrol these waters?"

"We have a small navy. They have a large one. Still, the ocean is bigger than both and the coastline very long." She smiled and took a sip.

"The driver of the moto volqueta is going home?"

She nodded and tapped her breast pocket where she kept a memory stick. "I will show these to my boss."

"Do you have an address for Brett Mara in Calgary?"

"What does RR mean on an address?"

Lane smiled. "He probably lives on an acreage. You will send me his address and his passport number?"

She nodded. "You will go after this man when you get back to Canada?"

Lane nodded in turn.

"And you will let me know if you find him so that he can be brought back here?"

"I will."

She stood up and handed him her card. "It is time for you to get ready for your niece's wedding." She picked up her cup and drained her coffee.

Lane sat, watched Deylis leave, then finished his coffee. The door to the bar opened and Gloria walked in with a young woman who looked to be fifteen or sixteen. The women turned. Gloria spotted Lane and smiled. She walked over.

"How are you?" Lane asked.

"You remember me now?" Gloria gripped her bottom lip between her teeth.

"I always remember you as you were. It took me some time to see you as you are. This is your daughter?"

A whisper of pain flashed across her eyes. "My niece, Ella. This is Paul Lane."

"He lived next door to you in the old house?" Ella looked at her aunt. The resemblance between the two was in the eyes and the chin. The niece had dark black hair, was taller than her aunt and weighed about the same.

Lane smiled.

"We should talk," Gloria said.

"Do you have any idea what they did to her?" Ella asked. Lane saw the rage in Ella's eyes.

Gloria took hold of Ella's elbow. Ella shook her off. "You lived next door. You must have seen something. Known something."

"He was a child. Maybe five or six."

My mother took a belt to me for asking about Gloria. After that I knew I couldn't trust anyone in my family. Lane watched Ella, then Gloria.

"Nobody helped her. Nobody cared what her mother did to her and the baby!" Ella was red in the face. She stepped closer to him.

Lane took a breath before he looked at Gloria. "Your mother killed the baby?"

The words came choking out of Gloria as she nodded. "She said it was for my own good, then told everyone it was crib death. What we now call sudden infant death syndrome."

"And she made your brothers bury the baby in the back-yard?" Gloria nodded.

Ella pounced. "Why did you do nothing?"

Lane kept watching Gloria, and when he spoke, his voice was as dead as the baby who was buried so many years ago. "I was six years old. I told my mother. She took a belt to me. The cries of the baby have haunted me ever since." *And the smell of death. I've been haunted by that, too.*

Gloria swiped her nose with a tissue. "They were good friends, our mothers."

Lane looked back at her but could think of nothing else to say.

"Her mother made it so she couldn't ever have children again!" Ella shouted. The women behind the bar turned to watch.

"What are you doing to him?" All heads turned to the woman in the doorway. Christine stood with her feet apart. Her hair was long and loose, her toes and fingernails were shiny blue and white tipped, and she wore white shorts and white blouse. She scanned the room as she moved closer. Her eyes locked on Ella and Gloria. "What are you doing to him?"

Lane stood up and put himself in front of Ella and Gloria. "Gloria is from my old neighbourhood."

"Why is that one yelling at you?" Christine's voice was low, dangerously slow.

Lane smiled. "Protecting her aunt, just like you are protecting your uncle."

Gloria asked, "Alison's daughter?"

"Yes. Christine, this is Gloria and her niece Ella. Gloria and I —"

"— had similar experiences growing up." Gloria shook Christine's hand. "Do you have time to sit down and talk with us?"

Christine looked at Lane. "You okay?"

"I'm fine." Lane looked at the women behind the bar, who were suddenly occupied in polishing the espresso machine. There were the sounds of the clinking of glass on ceramic and the low chatter of Spanish.

"You don't look fine." Christine looked sideways at Ella.

"We were catching up. They weren't exactly the good old days for either of us." Lane pulled out a chair and indicated Christine could sit if she liked. He sat down and Gloria sat down across from him. Christine remained standing across from Ella.

Gloria looked at Lane. "You are a homicide detective?"

Lane nodded. "How about you?"

Gloria looked at Ella. "It's okay. You can sit." She turned back to Lane. "I work at a bank."

"She's a manager." Ella sat down and looked up at Christine.

Gloria looked at Christine. "What is your mother up to?"

"She's locked up. It's where she belongs right now. My uncle and Arthur took me in when I got excommunicated from Paradise." Christine sat down.

Gloria leaned back as if to get a better look at Christine. "That's that polygamist community in the south of the province. Seems I read something a while ago in the newspaper about a woman from Paradise trying to abduct her daughter's baby. That was your mother?"

Christine raised her eyebrows. "That's her. Good ol' mom."

Ella sat up straight. "And I thought our family —" she pointed at her chest "— was fucked up."

Lane rolled his eyes and smiled. "Lots of people call them the good old days." He pointed at Gloria. "Not me, and I suspect not you."

Christine turned to Ella. "What happened in your family?"

"My grandmother killed my Aunt Gloria's baby, called it SIDS, made her brothers bury the body in the backyard and then had a doctor sterilize my aunt."

Gloria shook her head. "This isn't a contest to see who has the most messed-up childhood."

"I burnt down a house to escape Paradise." Christine gave Ella a look that said *I can match you at any game if you're going to mess with my uncle.*

"Okay if we dial down the estrogen just a bit?" Lane held his thumb and forefinger a millimetre apart.

Gloria smiled. "It appears you and I have been fortunate with our nieces. They are very protective and fiercely loving."

Change the subject. "Christine is getting married tomorrow."

Christine turned to face her uncle. "Are you going to be there?"

Lane found himself the focus of attention in the room. All sounds from the bar stopped and the three women at the table waited for his answer. He held up his hands. "By now the entire resort will be making sure I will be there. So chances of my not being there are remote."

Ella asked, "So, will you be there?" and laughed.

chapter 6

"Is Lola still saying the kids have to pay for the wedding?" Arthur stood in front of the mirror and did up the collar of his mauve shirt.

"I told the kids we would pay for it."

Arthur turned and looked at him. "When were you going to tell me this?"

"Now." Lane stepped into the closet to get his dress pants, which were hanging next to his blue shirt.

"Sure we can pay for it. I'd just like to be involved in the decision." Arthur flipped one end of his tie over the left shoulder.

"My apologies." Lane pulled on his grey pants.

"All will be forgiven as long as you are here for the entire day, don't get called away, do exactly what Christine asks you to do and pay one hundred percent of your attention to her." Arthur checked the knot of his tie in the mirror.

"What's your job?" Lane looked sideways at Arthur, then pointed. "To charm Lola and appeal to her vanities?" Lane fed his belt through the loops.

Arthur turned and smiled. "Actually, she was the one who went to charm school."

Lane laughed.

There was a knock at the door. Arthur reached over and opened it. Matt stepped inside with one hand holding his pants up. "You guys got an extra belt?"

Lane cocked his head to the left toward the closet. "I think so. It's hanging up in there."

"Any emergencies yet?" Arthur sat down to put his dress shoes on.

Matt shook his head. "Not yet. Okay if I come back in a few minutes with Indiana?"

"Has the surprise arrived yet?" Arthur asked.

"Nope." Matt left.

"The surprise was supposed to be here by now." Lane grabbed his shirt.

"This is Cuba, remember. Things seem to take the time they take." Arthur grabbed his jacket and hung it over the back of the chair.

They could hear the sound of footsteps pounding back and forth across the floor upstairs as Christine rushed to get ready.

Dan, Matt and Indy arrived at Lane and Arthur's room five minutes later. Indy was fast asleep in his tuxedo T-shirt, black onesie and black shoes. Dan, in his black suit, white shirt and black shoes, set Indie down in slow motion on the couch.

Matt hung his black jacket on a doorknob. "These clothes are gonna get real hot real quick."

Lane turned to Daniel. "How's Christine?"

Dan looked worried. "Running late. She wanted to feed Indy first and that took longer than planned. Did the surprise get here?"

Arthur and Lane shook their heads.

They heard the sound of high heels on the tiled floor above their heads.

Outside they heard a golf cart pull up.

Arthur peeked through the curtains. Dan looked over his shoulder. "The surprise made it."

They heard high heels climbing the stairs to the second floor. The second pair of heels stopped. The four men looked up at the ceiling.

Another pair of high heels tapped across the floor of the room above.

An instant of quiet, then a scream that reached out through the open sliding door to the room below.

Arthur said, "Now that is what I call timing."

"Alex always did know how to make an entrance," Lane said.

×

The wedding took place on a platform overlooking the beach at dusk. Christine wore a white form-fitting, mid-calf dress with a slit up the side to accentuate her long legs. The look was finished off with a pair of white stilettos and a black onyx pendant on a silver chain. With Christine between them, Lane and Arthur walked up the stairs to where Dan waited on one side of the Cuban equivalent of a justice of the peace named Laura. Matt, the best man, stood on the other side. He held the still-sleeping Indy. Alexandra stood on the right side of Laura. Alex wore the same dress as her sister, but in yellow, the same pendant, the same shoes and a smile that brightened the evening.

Christine reached the top of the stairs.

Lola looked back at the bride but did not smile. Her husband turned, saw Christine and did a double take.

When they arrived in front of Laura, Arthur sat down. Lane took Indy from Matt and sat down next to Arthur. Indy slept with the serenity only a child can manage at events minor and major. They watched as Laura raised her white-turbaned head, which matched her white flowing top and skirt, and began to speak. Her skin was almost the colour of the onyx the sisters wore. Lane began to smile as he thought, *I wonder what she would do if I told her about Lola's attempt to make Christine white?* He looked over at Lola and realized she must be thinking the same thing. Lola did something completely unexpected. She smiled nervously at Lane.

Later, at the dinner table in the Italian restaurant on the resort, Lane saw Christine was still smiling as she bent to kiss her son. She stood tall to kiss her sister's cheek, then leaned over to stroke Dan's cheek.

Deylis showed up thirty minutes later wearing a red dress, white pumps and a silver chain around her neck. She carried an acoustic guitar and was followed by a man with a cello. A woman trailed them with a pair of African drums.

Christine spotted the trio, frowned and looked at Lane.

Deylis smiled at the three and began to strum her guitar. It took a moment for the cellist and drummer to find chairs. They joined in and began to play a rumba.

Alexandra grabbed Arthur and they danced around the tables. Christine smiled and took Daniel's hand.

John stood up and tried to get Lola to do the same.

Lane got up with Indiana. The baby lifted one eyelid, then closed it again. Lane sat back down and watched. Dan and Christine danced as Deylis sang a Spanish love song. Alex and Arthur danced ballroom. Matt smiled, sat back and sipped a margarita.

Lola lifted her chin and marched away with her notice-me heels. As far as Lane could see, he was the only one who noticed.

John stayed. He sat alone for a minute, then got up, walked over and asked, "Mind if I join you?"

Lane shrugged. "Not at all."

John sat down. He looked at Daniel and Christine, then at Indiana. "The kids are having fun. I wish my daughter could have been here."

Lane waited while Indiana flexed his fingers.

"She works for an American company and they frown on anyone who goes to Cuba even now that the embargo's been lifted."

"Would you like a drink?" Lane asked as the waiter approached.

"Don't mind if I do." He turned to the waiter. "Mojito." The waiter nodded and turned to Lane.

"Same for me, please." Lane watched the dancing and listened to Deylis as she sang another Spanish song. *She has a beautiful sultry voice.*

John reached over and cupped Indiana's head with his hand. "Okay if I hold him?"

Lane nodded and began to lean forward. John did the same; then his phone rang. He held up one finger and reached for his cell. He looked at the screen, then said, "Yes?"

Lane recognized Lola's voice on the other end.

John nodded once and frowned. He took the phone away from his ear, pressed end and slid the phone into his jacket pocket. "I have to go." He got up, went to his son and daughter-in-law and hugged them both. Then he left.

Lane watched Daniel's shoulders sag. *I wonder what it was like for you growing up, Daniel?*

Christine hugged Dan and brought him over. "We wanted to thank you for the music. They're wonderful."

This is one of those times when everything just comes together. "It was a surprise to me just as it was to you."

Christine turned to watch the band, then turned back to Lane. "She did this because you helped her out?"

Lane shrugged. "You'll have to ask her."

chapter 7

"It was *fantastique*." Sylvie, a round-featured, dark-haired French woman, talked with her hands as Lane and Arthur sipped drinks at the outdoor bar near the fountain. Lane wore a Blue Jays ball cap, a long-sleeved shirt and shorts. Arthur wore much the same, except for the cap. His bald head was coffee-bean brown thanks to his Mediterranean ancestors.

Arthur looked at Lane. "Let's go swim with the dolphins. I've always wanted to do that."

"You will remember it for the rest of your life! Their skin feels like—" Sylvie looked around her, then rubbed her hand over the wet surface of the table where their cold drinks sweated onto glass "—like this."

"Can we go today?" Arthur asked.

Sylvie rubbed her fingertips on the v at the base of her throat. "You just rub a little chum right here and the dolphins come to you."

"Chum?" Arthur looked sideways at Sylvie.

Lane smiled while she frowned back. Sylvie said, "I don't know how to explain it."

"Fish guts," Lane said.

Arthur shook his head. "Maybe I'll just touch the dolphins."

Lane and Arthur headed for the Dolphinario an hour later in a blue-and-white 1955 Chev driven by Vlad, who appeared to be fluent in Spanish and English as well as an expert on baseball. Vlad opened the door, then offered, "I'll give you a free ride for the ball cap."

Lane shook his head, lifted the cap and said, "Keeps me from getting sunburned." Then he and Arthur climbed in the back seat, which was covered with some kind of vinyl. The springs sagged and groaned in much the same way the car did as it rolled down the highway, a loose assortment of parts all headed in the same direction.

They arrived at the Dolphinario and Arthur handed Vlad fifteen pesos. He smiled at the four-peso tip and held their door open. Three more tourists piled in and Vlad's smile broadened.

Inside the park they heard the clang of hammers against the metal framework supporting the stands facing the inlet. The water was lined by mangroves and fenced at intervals to hold and sort the dolphins. A welder worked at the base of the stands. Lane lifted his right hand to protect his eyes from the intense electric arc.

Arthur stood at the edge of the water and leaned on the railing as dolphins swam by. He was transfixed. Lane smiled and sat on the first bench. He looked out at the blue dock to the right side of the stands and the hoops suspended out over the water on the left. The stands began to fill up with families who mostly spoke Spanish. The clothing was different from what he saw at the resort. Most wore long pants, colourful sandals and shirts in various shades. *Must be the local people. This is kind of fascinating. I feel like I'm finally getting a glimpse at the people who actually live here.* He turned to watch his partner. *Arthur is like a child. He's mesmerized by the dolphins.* He spotted a flash of white out of his right eye. A man with a camera, telephoto lens and white golf shirt stretched over a generous spare-tire belly handed an envelope to another man. He wore a ponytail, a black ball cap and a shorty wet suit. Ponytail unzipped his wet suit and tucked the envelope up against his heart before pulling the zipper closed. *What did*

Angella say? Oh yes. Almost anything can be bought under the table in Cuba.

Ponytail opened the gate and stepped out onto the dock followed by a pair of female assistants in wet suits; they carried a pair of red coolers. Ponytail blew his whistle and the heads of five grey–blue dolphins popped out of the water and moved to the edge of the dock. High-pitched squeals began a chorus of demands until the trainers dropped fish into the mouths of the dolphins.

Arthur sat down next to Lane. There was a broad smile on Arthur's face as he watched the show. The dolphins propelled one of the trainers right up to the entrance to the dock. They flipped through the air, raced around the lagoon, leapt through the hoops and launched a female trainer up into the air. She somersaulted and dove into the water.

The show over, a small crowd gathered near the gate to the dock. The female trainers left with one of the coolers.

The photographer moved to the gate, allowed one person at a time onto the dock and took photographs.

Arthur was at the back of the line and needed a hand to make it across the gap between the dock and the gate. He walked over and knelt down next to Ponytail, who sat on the remaining red cooler. Arthur handed a five-peso note to the trainer, who blew his whistle. A dolphin rose up out of the water until he was nose to head with Arthur, who wrapped his arms around the creature and rubbed the top of the mammal's head. Lane took a series of photographs. The shutter of the nearby photographer's camera snapped, and then he gestured with his hand that Arthur's time was up.

Lane smiled as Arthur rubbed the head and the nose of the dolphin. Then the dolphin slipped back into the water and Arthur got to his feet. Arthur turned with a smile that reminded Lane of the intensity of the welder's torch when heat met metal.

Arthur's smile continued to illuminate the inside of the cab on their return to the resort. He leaned in next to Lane, then said simply, "Thank you."

It's been a long time since he's been so excited that he's at a loss for words. Cancer takes so much away. It's good to get something back.

×

The wind off the water tugged at Lane's shirt and shorts and pushed the waves up onto the sand. One wave broke, rolled up the beach and washed over his calves as he and Arthur walked side by side.

The water receded, and they looked into the distance where two women and two men walked toward them. Both women wore white shorts and white blouses over bikini tops. The men wore shirts and shorts. One of the men held a baby in the crook of his elbow.

Lane felt Arthur tuck an arm inside his elbow when they recognized the approaching group. They were deep in conversation. Matt said something. The others laughed. The sound was carried away by the wind. Christine looked up, saw her uncles and waved. They came to within an arm's length.

Another perfect moment. Enjoy it, because it won't last very long.

Christine put one arm around Arthur and another around Lane. She smelled of perfume, sunscreen, lime and tequila. "Thank you for this."

Matt said, "We're headed back for supper. Wanna join us?"

Alexandra stared at Arthur. "What are you smiling about? Get lucky?"

"He got to hug a dolphin." Lane felt his face redden.

"So he did get lucky!" Alexandra laughed.

"Just not the way you think," Arthur said.

"Well, are we or aren't we?" Christine asked.

"Are we what?" Dan asked.

"Going to get something to eat. I'm starved." Christine hefted Indiana. "And he will need a bottle." She began to walk back toward the resort. The rest followed as her long legs and natural grace attracted admiring glances from the men on the beach. The attention from the women varied from smiles to frowns.

Lane and Arthur's family walked up the beach, past the lifeguard and along the wooden walkway that tunnelled through the mangroves. They gathered around a column and washed their feet before following the sidewalk that wended its way between the clusters of buildings. They passed the pool, then reached the intersection in front of the hacienda-style buffet.

"I'm getting out of this damned communist country!"

They looked left.

Lola was dressed in yellow chiffon from cleavage to gold anklets. The wind tugged at the flowing fabric of her gown. She pulled a single silver carryon bag on wheels. Behind her came John with a pair of matching four-wheeled silver cases that reached to his belt. Each of the silver monsters appeared to want to go in a separate direction. Lola looked straight ahead as she crossed in front of Lane and headed up the sidewalk to reception.

"Was that a banana?" Alexandra asked.

John wore grey shorts and a green shirt and was red faced when he pulled up next to Dan. John tried to smile at his son but failed, then said, "The wedding, your room, it's all paid for." His shoulders sagged and he looked at his wife, who plowed through a dozen new arrivals with their luggage. "We said we'd pay for the wedding and . . ."

"John! We need to get to the airport!"

John leaned over and kissed Indiana on the cheek. He looked again at his wife, who stood eyeing him while she planted one fist on her hip. Lane saw John's pupils shrink into black holes. *He hates her!* Lane realized. John took a long breath, then pushed one bag forward and pulled the other along behind.

Alexandra looked at Lane. "You might have another murder to investigate before the day's over."

They walked up the steps to the red-roofed, cream-coloured building housing the buffet, went inside and found a table near the windows.

When they were seated, the waiter asked, "Would anyone like wine?"

Dan held up his glass. He looked out the window, shrugged, then reached for his son.

Alexandra asked, "Got anything stronger?"

chapter 8

Lori looked over from behind her computer. Her hair was blonder and her face was tanned so the smile creases at her eyes seemed white. "Did you bring pictures?" she asked as she leaned back in her chair.

Lane sat down in the chair next to her desk. His mind was fuzzy from yesterday's return flight. "I forgot."

Lori leaned forward, stood up, looked around to see if anyone else was about and handed him a bag. "For Christine and Dan."

Lane took the bag and looked inside. A deep-blue background was dotted with other vibrant colours on a hand-made quilt. "This is beautiful." He reached to pull the quilt out.

She touched his hand. "Quick. Go put it away. It's a special gift for your family. Trying to keep a secret from a bunch of detectives can be easy as long as you keep your mouth shut."

Lane stood up, walked over and kissed her on the cheek. She smelled of suntan oil and strawberries.

Lori blushed. "It's a good thing you're not in the RCMP or we'd both be in trouble."

Lane smiled and went into his office to tuck the package behind his desk. He came back out. "Can I get you a coffee?"

"Thought you'd never ask."

Fifteen minutes later, she sat in Nigel's chair sipping a cappuccino and Lane sat at his own desk slurping a moccaccino. Lori asked, "Lots of drama at the wedding?"

Lane rolled his eyes and nodded.

"Lola?" Lori crossed her left leg over her right and plucked at her ankle-length red skirt.

"I guess we should have realized when Lola said she'd pay for the wedding with no strings attached, she really meant that the wedding would be all about her."

"You mean it wasn't?" Lori smiled and set her cup down on Nigel's desk.

Lane swung his chair around to face her. He cradled his coffee in both hands. "Nope. Christine and Dan did get married after some drama. Indiana steals every show just by being Indiana. And then Dame Alexandra arrived."

"The southern belle made it, did she?" Lori nodded. "Lots more drama?"

Lane looked at the ceiling. "You know, I've been to gay weddings and straight weddings and I think this one was *the* most dramatic by far. Maybe that's why Arthur and I have never tied the knot — too much drama."

"Arthur can be pretty dramatic."

Lane looked at her and blushed.

"So you two are not going to tie the knot because of your aversion to drama?"

"Who's got an aversion to drama?" Nigel stuck his head inside the office.

Lori began to stand up. Nigel said, "Stay where you are."

Lane pointed at a cup on the corner of his desk. "That one's for you."

Nigel stepped inside wearing a purple shirt, black pants and black shoes. He took the cup and sipped. "Thanks. Did you get the messages from your old partner?"

Lane asked, "Harper or Keely?"

Nigel wiped his mouth with the back of his left hand. "Keely. She was asking if I knew what you were up to in Cuba. Said they were getting reports you were into something with the local police and some Cuban officials were checking up on you."

Lori turned to Lane. "So Lola wasn't the only one who was causing some drama."

Lane blushed. "It's not like I went looking for trouble."

"Are you going to fill us in?" Nigel asked.

"Actually I was going to ask for your help. A Brett Mara flew from Calgary to Varadero on WestJet. I need to know what you can find out about him." Lane wiped away the moisture gathering along his hairline on his forehead. *Why am I sweating?*

Lori stood up so Nigel could get at his computer. She moved to the chair tucked up against the wall. "Are you going to tell us or not?"

Lane took ten minutes to fill them in about the murder of Mara's wife Camille.

"So you think Mara came back here?" Lori asked.

Lane shrugged. "It's a possibility."

"Holy shit!" Nigel looked at Lane.

"What?" Lori leaned forward.

"This guy was a person of interest in a drive-by killing." Nigel turned his screen so that Lane and Lori could see a picture. "Is this him?"

Lane leaned over to look and nodded. "That's the guy. No fixed address, right?"

Nigel nodded. "That's right. Was a member of the FKs."

"Was?" Lori sounded surprised.

I thought you only left that gang when you're dead.

"According to this, he was a member of the FKs for ten years, was a suspect in two other drive-by shootings, then dropped out of sight." Nigel frowned at the screen.

"What?" Lane asked.

"Give me some time to look this over. This guy may have an alias or two."

Lori stood up. "I'll call the parole office to see if Lisa has any background on the FK connection. She's the one who usually deals with the gangs." She stepped out the door.

Nigel said, "You really know how to take a vacation."

Lane lifted his eyebrows, took a deep breath, exhaled slowly and said, "Cuba was full of surprises." The phone rang. He picked it up. "Lane here."

Lori said, "Lisa can meet you in half an hour at Higher Ground if you're buying."

Lane managed to make it to Kensington and found a place to park behind Pages Books. He parked beside a Volvo with LVS4VR on its licence plate. He went around behind the shops and walked down a metre-wide walkway between two buildings until he could see Kensington Road. He crossed the road and dodged a cyclist who ignored the fact that Lane was in the crosswalk. Then he walked east toward the coffee shop. Ahead, a group of four people and their dogs sat at the black metal tables and sipped iced lattes. At nine in the morning, the sun was already making the dogs pant. Their tongues dripped saliva onto the concrete. Lane went up the stairs and inside the coffee shop where painted mountain landscapes in rich colours adorned the walls. He spotted Lisa at a table up against one of the bay windows that looked out onto the street. She had long black hair and grey eyes and looked to be in her mid-forties. Lisa lifted her eyebrows, checked the collar on her blue blouse and waited. "What would you like?" Lane asked.

"A latte and one of their ginger cookies with the white icing, please." She smiled at him and Lane turned to order the coffees. He returned with a dessert plate bearing a cookie only slightly smaller than it. He sat down and she eyed the cookie. "I hear you want to know about Brett and the FKs." She crossed one leg over the other, leaned back and straightened her blue-and-red floral skirt.

"I was on a tour bus with him in Havana. His wife didn't make the return trip. Then she turned up dead."

"Brown hair, gathered at the back, flirty, liked to share her opinions with anyone in earshot?" Lisa asked.

Lane nodded.

"Her name was Camille Desjardin when I knew her."

"Large latte and large mocha for Lane!" the barista said.

Lane got up and returned with the coffees.

"Thanks." Lisa watched as he set the latte in front of her.

"How did you know Camille?" Lane sipped his moccaccino and smiled.

"She and Brett were boyfriend/girlfriend in high school. He got involved with the FKs and she told me she liked being a gangbanger's girlfriend because nobody would dare fuck with her and she got a nice car to drive." Lisa watched Lane's reaction to her tell-it-like-it-is approach with an intensity that made him look away and smile. "What's funny?"

"I'm usually the one doing the sizing up."

"Sorry. Occupational hazard. I needed to get out of there. One of the FOBs was shot outside my office last week. I must still be coming down from it."

"I'm just catching up on what happened while I was away."

"Word got out that Roland Lee was at my office, texts were sent and they were waiting for him when he left the building. Two shots to the head." She shrugged.

"Brett Mara was involved?"

She shook her head. "I don't think so. Brett dropped off the grid four or five years ago. His friend was killed in a drive-by. Brett was in the same car and must have figured he was next. I still get reports of sightings, but nothing solid. It's thought he and Camille are still together, though."

"Until about a week ago." Lane drank his moccaccino and marvelled at the magic of chocolate on the tongue.

"Lori said Brett is a person of interest in a killing. So it was Camille?"

"That's right."

"How did you get to be involved?"

"The Cuban police interviewed us all, then found out I was a homicide detective. We worked together a bit."

Lisa nodded. She frowned as she dipped the cookie into her coffee. She managed to get the soggy section of the cookie into her mouth before it disintegrated.

"Any idea what Brett is into now?"

"I did hear one rumour, but it was kind of out there."

Lane took a sip of coffee.

"One of my clients said that he saw Brett at one of those seniors residences."

"Did he mention which one?"

"Somewhere in the north. The client was a gang member who was visiting his grandmother. The client tried to get out of the gangs but was gunned down in a restaurant last month." Lisa looked at Lane and shrugged. "Sometimes the aftermath of this violence gets to me."

What do I say to that?

"I'll check with some of my contacts and see if I can get a line on Brett." Lisa dipped another corner of her cookie in the cup.

Lane looked out the window at the people and their dogs sitting near the sidewalk. *Most people live their lives without any firsthand experience of gangs or violence. Sometimes I wish I were one of them.*

×

Lane stepped back into the office. Lori was away from her desk. He stepped closer to the open door of the office he shared with Nigel, who was saying, "I'm not sure what time I'll get off work. Can I phone you when I know?"

Lane stepped into his office. Nigel leaned back in his chair, held his cell phone in his left hand and worked the computer mouse with his right. He lifted his chin in greeting to Lane, who sat down at his desk and switched on his computer. "Love you too," Nigel said and hung up.

"No." Lane felt a mixture of fear and anger boiling up inside of him. *Not this time. It's too dangerous.*

"What?" Nigel looked at Lane.

"You're not going to get Anna to help us track Mara down." Lane pointedly made direct eye contact with his partner. Anna, Nigel's girlfriend, had helped them in the past, although always unofficially.

Nigel looked away and fiddled with the collar of his shirt.

"Anna has been good for you, and I assume you've been good for her. Your style has certainly improved." Lane pointed at the colourful shirt Anna had bought for Nigel. "We're dealing with gangbangers. They have their own rules. They have eyes and ears in unexpected places. Some of them are cold-blooded killers. There are no rules as far as some of these guys go. If Mara or his buddies get an inkling Anna is looking into their operation, she'll be a target."

"It was about a post office box." Nigel scratched his cheek.

Lane waited.

"I've spent the last hour tracking down last known addresses and the one on his vehicle registration. They're all bogus. The only lead I have right now is a post office box. Anna was going to take a look."

Lane shook his head. "I said no. It could put her in danger. If you know where the PO box is, then we'll head out there and talk to the employees. I have a lead that Mara may be working at a seniors residence. We can work on both of those."

Nigel blushed.

"The last time I tracked down a gangbanger, he kidnapped Matt and Harper's little girl."

"You're joking!"

"Do I look like I'm joking?" Lane heard the quiet anger in his voice.

Nigel took a breath and released it slowly.

"Call Anna right now. I want to talk with her." Lane crossed his arms and waited.

Nigel picked up his phone and began to dial.

×

"Sorry it took so long. The longer I do this, the busier it gets." Harper came around from behind his desk and shook Lane's hand. "How was the wedding, and your holiday?" Harper wore his dress uniform. The jacket hung on the back of his chair. The top of his desk was scattered with multicoloured files. Lane could see Post-it notes stuck all around the edges of his computer monitor. He also saw that Cam's belly stretched tight against his belt and his hair was trimmed short, due, at least in part, to an ever-expanding bald spot.

Lane felt the firm grip of his friend's hand, squeezed back and smiled.

"Well?" Cam asked.

"The wedding went off with a hitch or two, but it went off." Lane smiled at the memory of the sun, Christine in her wedding gown and Indiana in his tiny tux.

Harper used his right hand to indicate that they should sit in the leather chairs arranged in a circle around a knee-high coffee table. "What happened?"

Lane sat. "Mother-in-law drama and a murder."

"Someone murdered Christine's mother-in-law?"

Lane laughed until he wheezed, then began to cough. "I'm sure that more than one person was tempted, but no, it wasn't her. Arthur and I went on a tour to Havana. One of the guys on the bus shoved his wife into what's called a moto volqueta. She died of head injuries. We were able to track down a photograph of the husband shoving her. The Cuban police have a copy of the photograph."

"What the hell's a moto volqueta?" Harper leaned back in his chair.

"Like a tiny dump truck with a box out front."

Harper tapped his fingertips together.

"The husband's name is Brett Mara. He used to belong to the FKs."

Harper leaned forward and his eyes narrowed.

"He left Cuba somehow, and we're working on the assumption that he's either back here or on his way."

"Any leads?"

Lane shook his head. "No fixed address."

"You need protection for your family." Harper stood up and went to his desk.

Lane nodded. *You don't need to remind him what happened last time.*

Harper picked up his phone and pressed a button. He looked at Lane.

This job has aged him.

"Mark? I've got a priority for you." Harper nodded at Lane. "I want twenty-four-hour surveillance for a homicide detective's home and family." He hung up. "Now you won't have to worry."

When it's family, you always worry.

×

Lane opened the door. Sam poked his nose around the corner, then moved into a downward dog. Even his tongue curled. Lane rubbed the side of the dog's head and scratched him behind the ear. Sam raised his right hind leg and scratched a rib. A clump of hair was dislodged and floated to the floor. "Come on outside!" Lane said and went to the back door so

Sam could shed in the yard. He closed the door and listened to the silence. Everyone must be asleep. *I wonder how long it will take for them to spot the unmarked vehicles?* He opened the fridge door, grabbed a sweating jug of lemonade and went looking for a glass. He could hear Arthur snoring as he drank the lemonade.

Sam scratched at the door. Lane opened it and Sam sat. Lane closed the door, put his glass down on the counter, went to the closet and grabbed the leash.

Five minutes later they were walking along a sidewalk running between backyard fences. They walked through an opening and followed the sidewalk that paralleled John Laurie Boulevard. Lane found his mind settling into the rhythm of the walk and began to relax. Traffic whispered by. A Jeep rolled by with its top down, a man driving and a pair of toddlers strapped into car seats in the back. A motorcycle crackled. Its rider wore a red mask over his face, a red helmet, red leather jacket and pants. His knees were at right angles from the gas tank. *Looks like Spider-Man.* A silver BMW sedan approached. Its windows were heavily tinted. The car slowed down and signaled a move into the nearest lane. Lane's breathing slowed. He waited for a window to roll down. He glanced left at the six-foot fence. He forced himself to take a slow, deep breath. The car rolled on by. Lane looked over his shoulder and watched the BMW stop at the traffic light. *Brett Mara doesn't know you exist. Keep it that way. No one in that car was trying to hurt you or your dog. Be ready for the real threats, not the imagined ones.*

chapter 9

"I've got a line on Brett Mara — or in this case, Brett Livingston." Nigel was waiting in the office with a set of car keys dangling between his thumb and forefinger.

Lane held the door to the office open, then followed Nigel after he walked through.

"On the hunt?" Lori asked.

Nigel waved at her as he said, "We're going to Floral Gardens on the east side."

It was a twenty-five-minute drive out of downtown, onto Memorial Drive, along the particular madness of Deerfoot Trail, turning east up the hill along the Trans-Canada Highway to the ever-expanding edge of the city. Lane spotted the building just beyond an overpass. The two-storey green-and-white structure was similar to a condo building or roadside motel. Nigel turned off the highway, along a two-lane road and then onto the driveway leading to a parking lot. The sign read *Floral Gardens Seniors Residence*. Nigel parked in the visitors parking. They got out and walked toward the automatic sliding doors and then were stopped by another pair of doors. Nigel held up his badge, pressed the button on the wall and waited as the receptionist looked up from behind her desk. The door slid open and she waited. Her hair was long, sleek and black. Her face was oval shaped, and her dark eyes watched them with minor interest. She flicked her hair over her shoulder revealing neon-blue nails. "Can I help you?"

Nigel tried to speak but croaked.

"We'd like to see the manager, please." Lane smiled.

"And who should I say is waiting?" The young woman lifted her phone and glanced sideways at Nigel, who blushed.

"Detectives Lane and Li." Lane looked at the lineup of seniors waiting patiently at the dining room doors.

"Two detectives to see you." The receptionist looked at her silver watch. Several gold bracelets jingled and she looked lazily at Nigel.

The time is displayed on her computer. Why is she looking at her watch?

She said, "It's five minutes before the doors open for breakfast."

They heard the click of heels on tiles, quickly muffled by carpet as a woman with shoulder-length blonde hair, a pin-striped suit jacket, a knee-length skirt and a blistering smile walked up to the detectives. She turned to the receptionist and said, "Thank you, Anita." The woman faced Lane and Harper, then extended her hand. "I'm Laura Mancuzi."

She has a firm, practised grip and manicured fingernails, maintains eye contact and smiles. I don't trust her.

"Follow me." She turned and walked past the line of seniors waiting for breakfast. "Good morning, Mr. Markham," she said as she passed a white-haired man leaning forward on his walker. A man about five metres away turned, looked at her with a wry sideways glance and said, "Markham was deaf as a post and he died last week!" Mancuzi didn't miss a beat as she walked down a carpeted hallway to a heavy wooden door.

This place is every shade of green, Lane thought as he followed her and noted the knots of muscle in the backs of her calves. *She either runs or works out.*

She opened the door. Her name was embossed in gold on the dark oak. "After you."

She waited for Lane and Nigel to sit down in a pair of heavy oak chairs before going to sit behind an oak desk the size of a queen-sized bed. "You have some questions."

Lane said, "We understand you have a Brett Livingston working for you."

"We did about six months ago." Mancuzi tapped her mouse and looked at her computer screen.

"Do you know where he works now?" Lane asked.

Tiny pressure lines appeared around Mancuzi's lips as she shook her head side to side.

"Do you have an address for him?" Lane asked.

Mancuzi looked at her screen, moved her mouse and tapped. "Twenty-six Canyon Crescent NW."

Nigel tapped at the screen of his smartphone as he wrote the address down.

"How long did he work here?" Lane asked.

Mancuzi lifted two freshly plucked eyebrows. "Two years."

"Was he close to any of the other staff?" Lane asked.

"Kept to himself," Mancuzi said.

"Could you give us any insight into why he left?" Lane asked.

Mancuzi looked at the ceiling. "I think he found a job closer to home."

Lane saw the line of sweat between the makeup on her forehead and her hairline. He stood up. Time to make a point. "A detective will contact you again tomorrow. At that time, you will be more forthcoming with information." He stood up and left the office.

Nigel hurried to catch up. "What was that all about?"

They passed though the foyer. Anita watched them with more than passing interest. The doors swished open. Lane turned right and headed for the Chev. He spotted a business card tucked under the windshield wiper. He walked over to the passenger side, took off his jacket and set it on the hood of the car. Nigel walked to the driver's side. Lane adjusted the collar of his shirt, picked up his jacket and the business card, then climbed inside. Nigel started the engine and they both opened their windows to let out the heat. Lane locked his seat belt and glanced at the card. "We have a meeting later today."

"Where?" Nigel looked over his shoulder as he reversed. "What the hell is going on?"

"Mancuzi was lying to us to protect her little empire."

"Okay. She was way too smooth. So, where are we going?"

Lane held the card between his thumb and forefinger. "A kitchen renovation company after we check Brett's address."

×

"This is the address Mancuzi gave us." Nigel checked the address he'd written down on his phone. "Twenty-six Canyon Crescent NW." He looked at the freshly poured basement. Parallel floor joists reached across the concrete walls. Nigel shifted into park and kept the air conditioning running. They looked at the houses on either side. One was numbered twenty-two and the other was thirty. "They look to be about fifty years old and nicely renovated." Mature trees grew in front of the neighbouring houses.

"We'd better check and see if the neighbours remember Brett." Lane opened his door.

"For all the good it will do," Nigel said.

In ten minutes they knew that neither of the neighbours had ever met Brett or Camille.

×

They found Phoenix Kitchens in Highfield behind a yellow refuse container the size of a wartime house. The one-time industrial area was being remodelled into a haven for small businesses and manufacturers.

"How did you know how to find this place?" Nigel nosed the Chev in on the right side of the container.

"Summer job." Lane got out of the passenger side and looked at the two-storey cinderbrick-and-glass building behind the yellow bin. There was a hollow *thunk* as someone on the roof of the building threw a piece of wood down into the container.

"Shit!" Nigel jumped at the sound, slipped around the front of the vehicle and looked up to see if there was any more incoming debris.

Lane looked at the front doors and saw a paper sign taped to the front door. An arrow pointed right. He walked over the fresh black pavement, up onto a concrete step, and opened the door. The drywall of the stairway was freshly taped and sanded, ready for paint. He went up the stairs to the second floor where a plywood floor spread out into something of an open office with second-hand furniture occupying four corners of the room. At each desk sat one person. Each had black hair. Each wore casual clothing. Only one made eye contact with Lane. The man looked to be about thirty, was over six feet tall, had neatly trimmed black hair and wore a blue golf shirt and navy-blue slacks. He stood up from behind his desk, walked toward Lane and extended a hand. "Welcome to Phoenix Kitchens. Sorry about the mess. I'm Neville."

Lane shook Neville's hand. "Anita asked us to meet with her."

A voice carried down the hallway to their right.

Nigel shook Neville's hand and turned at the sound of the voice on their right.

Lane gripped his earlobe and made eye contact with Nigel. *He's got it.* It was their signal for Nigel to pretend that he couldn't understand what was being said. Lane guessed that the voice in the hallway was speaking Cantonese or Mandarin.

Anita stepped out into the hallway followed by a shorter woman wearing black pants and a top made of colourful red fabric bought on sale and sewed at home. She was at least sixty and looked at the detectives with frank distrust.

Anita said, "These are the men who came to the ask questions at Floral Gardens. This is my Aunt Rose."

Aunt Rose stepped into the middle of the room. Even though she was a head shorter than anyone else, she was obviously in charge. The others deferred to her. It was written all over their body language as they took a step back or lowered their eyes. Rose crossed her arms under her breasts.

Lane looked around. The other women were on their feet and gathered in a loose circle around them. He turned to Anita and waited.

Anita turned to Neville, who said, "We heard you are looking for Brett Livingston."

Lane nodded. "That's correct."

Aunt Rose used heavily accented English when she said, "That evil shit killed my mother!"

One of the other women waited for a nod from Rose before she said, "Our grandmother died at Floral Gardens. They said it was a heart attack."

Another said, "She was born in China and could speak only a few words of English. Before she died she was nervous and upset but wouldn't talk about it. After she died we found this."

Anita handed over a note. Lane looked at the column of characters and handed it to Nigel.

Aunt Rose said something that sounded like a curse to Lane. He only recognized *gwai lo*.

Anita frowned. "The note says that my brother was broke and in jail in China. He didn't want to tell his parents about it so he was asking my grandmother for money."

Neville said, "After she died there was fifty thousand dollars missing from her bank account."

"Brett the pig killed Ayah!" Aunt Rose said.

"When Anita asked her boss about it, Brett disappeared and it all got swept under the carpet by Ms. Mancuzi," Neville said.

Anita put her hand on Aunt Rose's shoulder. "Mancuzi said we had no proof, that Brett was gone and it would only upset people. She said we had to learn to accept that Ayah was dead and that accepting death is difficult sometimes. I found out later that Mancuzi gets a bonus every year if the Gardens stay full. She's afraid she'll lose her bonus if word gets around that Brett killed Ayah and stole her money."

Aunt Rose held up three fingers. "Three wars! Ayah live through three wars, then die in Gardens!"

Neville said, "Ayah worked her entire life. Raised two kids on her own after her husband was killed when the Japanese invaded. Got them out of China when Mao had his Cultural Revolution, brought them to Canada and put them both through university. She was a remarkable woman."

Anita put her arm around Aunt Rose's shoulder. "If you find this Brett Livingston, we want to know what he says happened to Ayah."

Lane nodded and looked back at Rose, who refused to blink. He handed his card to Aunt Rose and Neville. "If you think of anything else or discover where Brett Livingstone is, contact me right away."

Ten minutes later, as they drove down Blackfoot Trail with the fairgrounds in the foreground and the city centre in the background, Lane asked, "What was Aunt Rose saying?"

Nigel smiled. "That she didn't think the police would be any help and Brett would get white justice."

"White justice?"

"She thinks you and I are crooked because we're police. The police she's used to dealing with were almost always corrupt."

✕

Walter Riley sat in his wheelchair in the sunroom at Bowmont, a seniors residence where those who'd managed to hold onto their minds lived on the main floor and those who hadn't lived on the second. There the doors and elevators had key codes to keep all the lost minds in one place.

Green and yellow budgies in a cage about three metres away were happily chatting in the sunlight. Walter looked at the cafeteria clock and saw it was an hour until dinnertime. He patted his stomach with the palm of his right hand, the only hand he could move with any kind of accuracy even though the fingers were slow to obey him.

A woman screamed on the second floor. It was a wild, haunting sound. Walter saw heads turn and look up at the balcony. He thought, *One good thing about being deaf is that I can barely hear the howling anymore.*

The new nurse in flashy royal-blue top and pants walked past. His name tag said Brett.

Walter's reaction was immediate. His bowels clenched as if some mighty hand had reached into his abdomen, gripped his large intestine and squeezed. That was followed by shortness of breath as his diaphragm pressed against his lungs. He heard Kaye, his ten-years-dead wife, say, "How do you know? How can you possibly know that?" And he would try to explain that after his first fifteen years of teaching, his body had recognized the signs from a person's body language. He just knew. The words from *Macbeth* came to him like a fish rising lazily to the surface of the lake to swallow a duckling: *By the pricking of my thumbs, something wicked this way comes.* Even though he was deaf, had lost almost everything but his mind, his sight, his memories and his appetite, he knew that Brett was a predator.

✕

Christine was waiting with Indiana and Sam when Lane got home. "I need to go for a walk." She handed him a sandwich in a plastic bag.

"Can I lose the tie and put on my other shoes?" Lane hung his jacket in the closet.

Christine frowned. Lane took a long slow breath, then grabbed the leash in one hand and the sandwich in another. He waited as she grabbed the diaper bag and Indiana. Lane followed her out the kitchen door and onto the deck where she snapped Indiana into the stroller and stuffed the bag into the carrier under the baby. Lane put the leash on Sam and kept the sandwich out of the dog's reach.

They walked along a street with single-family homes on either side. Every so often a metal container stood out front of a house being renovated. Lane still had a mouthful of tomato, lettuce, cucumber and soy cheese (becoming a mother had transformed Christine into a health food advocate) when Christine said, "Dan is sad because of what happened at the wedding. He's worried about his dad."

Lane covered his mouth with his fist. "Where is Dan?"

"Asleep. He's back working on the golf course. Starts at five tomorrow morning." Christine looked under the stroller's visor to see that Indiana was checking whether his toes would fit in his mouth.

"Lola isn't going to change." Lane stuffed the remains of the sandwich in his mouth and the bag in his pocket.

"He knows that!"

Sam turned his head and looked at Lane. *Don't worry, you won't need to run and hide.*

"Dan would like to have a relationship with his dad, that's all."

They turned a corner and headed west toward the Rockies. The mountains were hidden behind rows of two-storey houses. "He could go downtown to meet his dad for a coffee some afternoon. Dan gets off work at two, doesn't he?"

Indiana began to fuss. Christine stopped, fished a bottle out of the bag and handed it to the baby. "Is coffee your solution to everything?"

"Did you bring me on this walk to talk or to fight?" *Now you've done it!*

Christine's face turned red. Sam darted left to escape and nearly yanked Lane off balance.

"I'm just worried about him," Christine said.

"John likes to golf. Maybe they could go golfing. That way they can talk and relax at the same time."

Christine looked ahead and waved.

Lane followed her gaze and spotted Donna sitting in a lawn chair in the shade at the mouth of her garage. A playpen was next to her and an infant was visible through the mesh. It lay on its back attempting to roll over. "Pull up a chair and join me for a lemonade?"

Christine looked at Lane, who said, "Sure." *Anything to stop the interrogation. I have no idea how to fix Dan's problem with his parents.*

Sam followed them past Donna's pickup and into the shade of the garage where her Harley was attached to a sidecar with a baby car seat strapped inside.

"You let the baby ride in there?" Christine asked as she picked up Indiana, cradled him in her right arm, then sat next to Donna in a lawn chair.

"Not yet. Maybe at the end of this summer or next. I just want to be ready when she is." Donna had her brown hair cut short. She reached over and poured lemonade from a jug into a pair of glasses. She handed one to Christine and another to Lane. "What's new? Haven't talked to you two since before Lisa was born." She raised her glass.

Lisa? Wasn't that the name of your sister who was killed in Afghanistan? Lane took a sip. "This is delicious. What's your secret?"

"Fresh lemons and raw sugar." Donna smiled.

"I got married last week in Cuba." Christine flashed her new white-gold wedding band.

Donna reached over to inspect the ring. "Very nice. How was Cuba?"

"The beach was amazing. The wedding was..." Christine glanced at Lane.

"Christine looked fabulous as always. Her sister managed to get there even though she lives in the States. Indy wore a tux." Lane inched closer to Sam, who groaned and sat.

"My mother-in-law thought it was all about her. Then my uncle got tangled up in a murder investigation." Christine shook her head.

Donna smiled. "Sounds like a wedding to remember. When do I get to see the pictures?"

We've been looking for Brett while we should have been looking for the women Camille talked with.

Christine said, "How about if I bring them around tomorrow after supper?"

chapter 10

"I'm trying to get a hold of Lisa. You have a message from a Gloria." Lori held up her hand with a written note. Lane grabbed the note as he walked past her desk and into his office. He sat down, picked up his phone and dialed.

"Hello?" A woman's voice asked.

"It's Paul Lane."

"Thank you for calling me back. I hope this isn't a bad time."

"Go ahead." He leaned back in his chair.

"I would like to give my baby a proper burial. I know it's an unusual request. You're the only one who has any understanding of the situation and might be able to tell me where to start or who to ask."

Lane winced at a childhood flashback of his mother taking the belt to him. "Was it a homicide?"

"Yes. My mother admitted that she smothered my baby." Her voice was as empty as a rain barrel in the middle of a summer drought.

"I need you to come in and do some paperwork. Then I'll contact a friend who may be willing to do the exhumation." *How come you sound so clinical? Gloria has been living with this as long as you have. It has left a stain on both of our lives.* "I'm sorry. Could we discuss this over a cup of coffee? How about tomorrow morning, early?"

"Where and when?"

He told her and hung up.

Lori stood in the doorway and waved a piece of paper at him. "I've got a name and number for you. From now on you contact Lisa through me. She's taking a week off. She can't shake the shock of the shooting that happened outside of her building." She handed the note to Lane. "Christy Mackenzie called. She says she was friends with Camille."

×

Nigel took time to track down background information on Christy Mackenzie, who lived at the ever-expanding southern edge of the city and worked downtown within five blocks of Lane's office. They walked east along 6th Avenue to The Bow. Fifty-eight floors of crisscrossed steel, curved glass and concrete in the shape of a bow. "She works for Encana." They rode the elevator to the eighth floor and asked the receptionist to see Ms. Mackenzie.

They sat in plush comfort for five minutes until a woman dressed in a pale-blue jacket with matching skirt and navy-blue heels came to fetch them. "Christy Mackenzie." She reached out her hand and shook with a wiry grip.

"Thank you for seeing us on such short notice." Lane followed her down the corridor. He watched her shoulder-length blonde hair swing from side to side as she walked. She stopped in front of an open door, then held her left hand out for them to go in first. She shut the door behind them.

"I heard about what happened to Camille." She sat down behind a glass-topped desk, crossed her left leg over her right and straightened her skirt. Christy raised her brown eyes and looked right back at them.

She definitely has the no-nonsense approach down pat. "We understand that you might be able to provide some background on Brett Mara."

Christy nodded at the detectives. "Camille was my cousin. We went to the same high school."

You must know about the FKs as well.

"We're trying to contact her husband," Nigel said.

Christy leaned her head to the right and studied the younger detective. "That son of a bitch Brett killed her, didn't he?"

That façade sure left in a hurry. Lane said, "He is a person of interest in the investigation into her death. We are trying to locate him."

Christy shook her head and made a backhanded swipe at her eyes, then reached for a tissue. "We knew it. Brett was a gangbanger from way back, and she wouldn't listen to any of us when we tried to tell her what he was like."

"It happened in Havana," Lane said.

"I saw her a week before she left. She was looking forward to the trip. Said she was thinking of leaving him. There was this new guy. She said she had stuff on Brett that made him easy to manipulate." Christy dabbed at the corners of her eyes.

"We would like to talk with Brett," Lane said.

The sound Christy made was somewhere between a cough and a laugh. "Good luck. The only way Camille and I could stay in touch was when she would call me once every two weeks or so. Her phone number always came up as unknown. That's how I would know it was her. We would always meet at the mall or a restaurant, never at her place."

"Do you have the name of the new guy?" Nigel asked.

Christy shook her head. "She did say it was a friend of Brett's, but she wasn't worried because she could blow the whistle on Brett's latest scam and then he would end up in jail. In fact I think she was planning to do exactly that."

"Did she give you any information on the scam?" Lane asked.

"She said something about old people and their grand-children. She started to explain the last time we met. Then her phone rang and she had to leave. She said she would fill me in when she got back. There was something she wanted to take a look at in Cuba, a property, I think."

"Do you know anyone who might be able to help us locate Brett?"

Christy looked at her cell phone set to the right of her keyboard. She picked it up and pressed a button then flipped through two pages of apps. "Carlo."

"Carlo?"

Christy turned the phone so they could see it. There was a picture of a truck with *Carlo's Calzones* written across the top. "Talk with Carlo. He contacted me and was looking for Brett."

×

Carlo's truck was glacier blue. The blue Lane had seen just once at Moraine Lake a thirty-minute drive away from the more famous Lake Louise. *Thankfully he didn't put a calzone on the truck. It would have looked—*

"Obscene. The calzones are supposed to be so good, it's—" Nigel looked at the face of his phone. "The guy scores ninety-five percent on customer satisfaction."

Carlo's name was written in green above the open windows. Below that, a horseshoe of mountains cradled a glacier. *It* is *Moraine Lake.*

A voice from inside the truck asked, "What's your pleasure, gentlemen?"

"Two calzones. Two coffees." Lane handed over a twenty and got back a toonie and two loonies. He dropped a loonie in the tip cup and pocketed the rest.

"Name?" the voice asked.

Lane saw the shadow of a person inside. *How does a guy that size move around in there?* "Lane."

"Ten minutes." A hand the size of a spaghetti bowl handed over a napkin. Lane stuffed it in his pocket.

Nigel handed one coffee to Lane. He stepped aside to open the way for the next in line and said, "I've been wanting to try out this one. It's becoming a bit of a legend around town. Some of the complaints from the established restaurants have gotten louder. They say the food trucks are hurting their business. Now we can find out for ourselves."

Lane watched the lunch crowd checking their watches and phones, rolling up wrappers, grabbing pop cans then lining up to drop the recyclables in their proper containers. Nigel leaned closer. "Think we look like cops?"

Lane smiled, looked at his right hand and spotted a note written in black on the napkin. "He'll meet us after the lunch crowd leaves. Christy must have called him." Lane sat down across from the cast sculpture of the chess player who stared forever at the pieces on the table.

"Think he's winning?" Nigel sat next to the statue.

"No idea. I'm not much of a chess man."

"That's funny. Sometimes you make me think you're working several moves ahead."

Lane shook his head. He turned as a diesel pickup parallel parked a couple of cars ahead of the calzone truck. The engine clattered off, the doors opened and a pair of alligator boots was followed by Wrangler jeans, a leather belt with a Stampede belt buckle, a white shirt with silver buttons, a black cowboy hat and a tanned face with a five o'clock shadow. The driver came around the front of the truck, stepped up on the curb and put his hands on his hips. He was dressed in black from cowboy boot toe to crown. He slapped his friend on the back. "Hey, Ronnie, let's get us a calzone."

Nigel heard the accent, spotted the white outline of Nova Scotia on the rear window of the pickup, then said just loud enough for his partner to hear, "East Coast cowboys."

Lane shook his head as the pair sashayed their way up to Carlo's truck. Ronnie reached into his shirt pocket, pulled out a fifty and said, "Couple of calzones for me and Blair."

The fifty disappeared; the massive hand reappeared with the change. Ronnie said, "Thanks, pardner."

Nigel chuckled. "It's fuckin' ridiculous what people from the rest of the country think they know about this town."

Lane smiled as he watched the East Coast cowboys stand with hands fisted on their hips. The cowboys kept checking to see who was watching.

"Lane!" A man appeared at the passenger door of the food truck. His hair was black, his face was angular and he filled the interior of the cab.

"How does that guy move around inside of that truck?" Nigel asked.

Lane shrugged, got up, walked to the open door, took the paper-wrapped calzones, thanked the man with biceps the size of cured hams and returned to the chess man. He handed one of the calzones to Nigel.

"You're awfully quiet." Nigel peeled back some of the paper until one tip of the calzone was accessible.

"Thinking." Lane unwrapped the top half of his calzone and bit. The blend of flavours — spiced Calabrese salami, tangy tomato sauce and melted buffalo mozzarella wrapped in pita bread — wiped every other thought from his mind.

"This is amazing," Nigel said between bites.

Lane took another bite. Less bread meant more of the meat and sauce combination intensified the experience.

"*Partyinthemouth*." Nigel's mouth was full and the words were garbled into something vaguely obscene.

"Who you talkin' 'bout?" Ronnie the cowboy moved to stand over Nigel.

Lane looked at the anger in Ronnie's face and saw that Blair had his friend's back. Lane spotted the hearing aid in Ronnie's ear. The detective set his sandwich down and swiveled to face the pair. He stood up and wiped his lips with a napkin, then held out his hands. "A misunderstanding."

"I'm talkin' to him." Ronnie pointed at Nigel and moved closer.

This would be laughable under normal circumstances, Lane thought as he caught the stink of rye whiskey on Ronnie's breath.

"Blair! These are yours!" Everyone within half a block turned as Carlo stepped off the truck with a calzone in each hand. He was six feet tall and three feet wide. His brown eyes were black with foreboding.

The man is built like a brick. Carlo dwarfed the pair of cowboys as he handed them their calzones. He lifted his chin. "Who's driving?" He looked at Blair.

"I am." Blair reached into his pocket and pulled out his keys.

"Good. See you next time." Carlo watched them walk over to the truck and climb inside.

Carlo turned to Lane and Nigel. "Christy said you guys wanted to talk with me about Brett."

"That's right." Lane slid over to one side of the bench so Carlo could sit down. Still, Carlo's shoulder rubbed up against Lane's.

The pickup started up. The trio turned as the super-charged diesel wheezed, the tires spun and Ronnie flipped them the bird out the rear window, his finger framed inside the white outline of Cape Breton.

"Fuckin' guys wouldn't know which end of a horse was which. All they'd be good at is fallin' off." Carlo waved as the truck farted black smoke, the rear wheels shuddered and the pair pulled away.

"These calzones are awesome." Nigel held up his and smiled.

Carlo smiled back. "My grandmother taught me how to make them from scratch. From dough to sauce and everything in between."

"You're lucky," Nigel said.

"I know. She saved my life. Then Brett killed her after he got nearly fifty-five thousand out of her bank account. I went to Cancun for a holiday. Brett told her I had been arrested in Mexico and needed money to get out of jail. The day I got back, my grandmother was found dead. They said it was heart failure, but it wasn't. Brett was covering his tracks. It was just too much of a coincidence that she died when she did. She would have talked to me about him. He must have known it so he killed her and then moved on."

"Do you know of any other seniors residences where he worked?" Nigel asked with thumbs at the ready to enter the information on his phone.

Carlo lifted his left hand and counted off fingers with his right. "The Point in Edgemont, Floral Gardens on the east side, Buena Vista in the south, Scenic Settings in the west."

"Who did you talk with?" Lane asked.

"You gotta understand, most of the seniors homes are owned by an outfit down east. They're tomato counters." Carlo exhaled slowly.

"Tomato counters?" Nigel looked up from the keyboard on his cell phone.

"Some guy down east decides they're spending too much on food so the residents are told they can have only one cherry tomato per salad." Carlo made eye contact with Lane. "I have kitchen connections. They tell me how things work."

Lane lifted his chin. "You said your grandmother saved your life."

Carlo nodded. His neck was as wide as his head. "When I was sixteen I was hanging around with Brett and some of the FKs. My aunt's cousin was the resource officer at the school. She told my grandmother. She took me out of school and put me to work at the restaurant for a year. I worked six days a week for ten months. Then she put me into Saint Francis where I could play football and the family could keep an eye on me."

"The family?" Nigel asked.

"Francis has lots of Italians. My grandmother has some connections. They watched who I was hangin' with. After high school, she sent me to university where I played some more football and got my master's."

Nigel opened his eyes and pointed. "You were drafted into the CFL."

Carlo nodded.

"What was your major?" Lane asked.

"MBA."

Nigel asked, "How come you never played in the CFL?"

"My grandmother had seen other guys from Francis go pro and they all got pretty banged up. One still has problems with concussions. She said I would do better with my own business." He pointed at the truck. "She bought it for me. Her restaurant did well."

"These other places where Brett worked, what did you find out?" Lane took a sip of coffee and another bite of calzone.

Carlo leaned his head to the right. "Brett would arrive — you have to understand these places are crying for qualified staff — and charm everyone. Then a handful of seniors would get real quiet, some of the staff would get suspicious, there would be a cluster of deaths, usually attributed to heart attacks, and afterward some of the families would show up asking about money missing from their parents' bank accounts."

"Did you get a line on anyone working with Brett?" Lane asked.

"There is a rumour..." Nigel began.

Lane looked at Nigel. *Wait!*

"I'm not talking about rumours. I'm talking about what I know. Are you guys serious about this case? I mean, are you going to arrest Brett and then back off or are you going to fuckin' solve this case?"

Lane looked right at Carlo. "We want to solve the case."

Carlo looked around to see if there was anyone within earshot. "One of the FKs has something on an MLA. There is a private member's bill before the legislature. It would allow a company from the States to open a couple of seniors homes. A few of the FKs want to move to Cuba. The first part of their plan is to invest in this American company. Then they can go to Cuba and live off the profits from their investment. It's like freedom thirty-five for gangbangers."

"How come you're telling us all of this?" Lane asked.

"Christy told me you were asking around and she told me what happened to her cousin. I figure that if you find Brett before I do, it'll save you tracking me down for murder."

Lane laughed even though he knew Carlo wasn't joking. He lifted the calzone. "Just when I was starting to enjoy this. I want to be able to come back for more."

Carlo slapped his hands on his thighs and stood. He reached into his pocket and handed Lane a card. "In case you need to get in touch."

Lane pulled a card out of the inside of his jacket pocket with his left, took Carlo's card with the index and forefinger of his right. Then he stood up and moved closer to the man. "If you hear where Brett is, then let me know right away. I want you to be able to go back to Moraine Lake whenever you want."

Carlo studied the detective for several seconds. "You're the first person who recognized my favourite spot. Used to go there with the family for barbecues. My grandmother really knew how to do pork ribs on a wood fire."

"Call me first," Lane said.

Carlo nodded, then walked back to the truck.

×

Walter watched the Blue Jays turn a double play. The short-stop scooped up a grounder and in one graceful motion flipped the ball to the second baseman, who tagged the base and leaped into the air to avoid the sliding runner. In mid-air, the second baseman threw the ball to first in time to beat the hitter. The runner slid face first into the base a tenth of a second too late. Walter lay in his bed and waited for the slow-motion replay. After yesterday's shock, he needed to rest and recoup after lunch.

He looked over at Marvin, who was dying. They had a dove over his name outside the door. Every morning and evening the nurse would come to give Marvin a pain patch. Walter wondered if it was to make it easier for Marvin and his pain or easier for the staff because Marvin was more compliant when he was drugged. *At least he's not pissin' all over the bathroom,* Walter thought. Marvin's Parkinson's had caused him to piss more in the general direction of the toilet than in it. *The guy couldn't hit the broad side of a barn.*

He spotted the approaching spring-loaded clogs. It was one of the things he'd noticed about Brett. That and the royal-blue pants and shirt. No one else in the institution wore either those shoes with the springs in their heels or that shade of blue uniform. Walter let his upper eyelids drop eighty percent of the way to his cheeks and waited.

Brett entered the room, glanced at Walter and then the TV. He walked to the window near the empty bed. Walter knew that Marvin's bed would soon be taken by someone new. His only hope was that the new guy's aim was better.

Brett turned from the window and stood next to Walter. He saw the hand reach for his orange juice. When the glass reappeared it was a quarter full. Brett gave Walter a predatory tap on the shoulder. The old man concentrated on remaining still until Brett left the room.

Walter opened his eyes in time to see the Blue Jays' centre fielder stretched out at the warning track. The ball disappeared into the centre of his mitt. Then he slid in the sand and rolled onto his back with the glove held up and the ball inside. *Anticipation. That is the key. Anticipation, focus and patience*, Walter thought.

The germ of a plan formed in his mind. He felt alive for the first time in months and hoped the feeling would last long enough for him to die feeling that way. He looked over at Marvin and saw the skeleton that once was a man. Someone who had gone to war, survived, come home, raised a family and worked for over forty years. *A dog wouldn't be allowed to suffer like this. Why treat Marvin worse than a dog?*

chapter 11

They watched a young woman cross the street. She wore a red dress made of sheer fabric. The sun shone down the street to reveal her black thong.

Gloria wore blue shorts, a white long-sleeved blouse and sandals. She asked, "Were you ever young and unaware?"

Lane thought about her question as he sipped his coffee. They sat outside at a round black metal table. It was a rare morning with the cool promise of plus thirty by noon.

She smiled. "I can't remember either."

Gloria seems to want to talk, so let her talk. He took another sip and watched her as she turned to face him. *I wonder how she managed to hang onto her kindness after what her mother did to her?*

"Looking after my baby's remains has been on my mind for many years. I was taught that she couldn't go to heaven because she wasn't baptized. I don't believe that anymore." She frowned at the coffee in her paper cup as if it might help her to find the right words.

Lane waited.

"Seeing you in Varadero brought back so many of those memories."

Lane nodded. *We are both haunted by memories of that time.*

"When I talked with Arthur, I found out you were also scarred by what happened to my baby."

"You talked with Arthur?" Lane felt perspiration gathering under his arms and it wasn't just because of the sun's hand on his back.

"Yes. You were in Havana or Matanzas and I was having a margarita. He joined me and we began to talk."

Lane lifted his chin. *How come you didn't tell me, Arthur?*

"I thought that if my baby received a proper burial, maybe we could both feel a bit better about what happened." She raised her eyebrows as if inviting a response.

"What can you tell me about how the baby died?"

Gloria looked out at the cars passing on the street. "I woke up after my mother had said she would look after my baby. When I got up my mother said the baby had stopped breathing. She said that happened to some babies. My mother told my brothers to bury her in the garden. I was crying. She told me to shut up, that I'd gotten myself into this mess and she would deal with it."

"You said before that the child was murdered."

Gloria nodded, turned to Lane and began to speak in a voice devoid of emotion. Its lack was revealing. "We put my mother in a home a few years ago. She was suffering from dementia. She started to talk about the baby girl she smothered and then had buried in the garden."

Lane lifted his chin. *How did you survive?*

"It's funny." Gloria made an attempt to smile. "I often wondered if you would survive. You were nothing like anyone else in your family. Your sister and brother tormented you constantly, and your mother —"

"Was much like your mother." *Now my voice has gone monotone.*

"I've done a lot of reading. I took classes at the university, mostly psychology. Hoping they would help me figure it all out. I came to the conclusion that you and I were in the same boat. We both had mothers who were sociopaths."

She looked across the street at a cyclist who carried a clear plastic bag of cans and bottles slung over one shoulder. He swerved in between and around pedestrians. "How come we didn't end up living on the street?"

Lane smiled and shrugged. "Just lucky, I guess."

"I drove by the old house. There is still a garden in the backyard. I know where my baby is buried."

Lane nodded. "I'm going to need to talk with your brothers."

"To verify my story?" Gloria crossed her arms under her breasts.

"That, and for your protection."

Gloria lifted her chin and frown lines appeared above her nose.

Give her a minute to put it together.

"That way I can't be charged with murder?"

"That's correct."

"That thought hadn't even occurred to me."

Lane lifted his coffee with his right hand and raised his eyebrows. "That's because you're not in my line of work."

"When and where do you want to meet my brothers?"

"Here," Lane put the flat of his right hand atop the table. "This time tomorrow if possible. Do they still live in town?"

She nodded. "Yes. Yes, they do."

"Will you let me know if they can meet? Earlier is better."

"You haven't asked her name."

Lane frowned and waited.

"Christine. Her name was Christine."

It took Lane a moment before he was able to think. *What would have happened to my Christine if Arthur and I hadn't been there?*

×

"I've been checking out Mi Casa Su Casa seniors residences. Someone has set up a site that lists the problems family members and residents have had with the company." Nigel sat back and sipped the latte Lane had set in front of him.

Lane sat at his desk. "Is that the company from the States that's trying to get into Alberta?"

"Yes, and it looks like they run quite the scam. You pay for your suite like you pay for a condo. Then after you die, the property reverts to MCSC. Residents still pay money each month for any and all services. Nobody in their right mind would buy into this." Nigel pointed at the screen as he took a sip of coffee.

"Maybe the people who do sign up aren't in their right minds."

"This MCSC business model is structured to rip off old people every time they get up in the morning. It rips them off even if they don't get up some morning."

"If Carlo is right, then that's why Mara was looking to buy in. The return on his investment would be very high."

"So high that he could live on a tropical island, and live very well."

Lane nodded. "Like Cuba." *So it's just another scam, only this one involves murder. I wonder if we'll ever know how many victims there have been.*

"Or Mexico, or even the Bahamas."

"Who's the politician behind the private member's bill?"

"Bill Rogerson," Nigel said.

Christ! The solicitor general. Lane leaned forward. "We need to talk with Harper."

✕

Ninety minutes later they sipped coffee and waited in Harper's office. Lane looked out at the blue prairie sky, the river valley and the towers. The door opened, Harper rushed in and the door closed behind him. "What's up?" He tossed his cap onto the shelf next to the window. His face was lean, his head was shaved and he'd lost the moustache. He shucked off his uniform jacket, hung it on the back of his chair and sat down.

"We need to bring you up to speed on a new case." Lane put his coffee down and saw Nigel reach for the folder of information on the coffee table.

"Go." Harper shook his head, got up from behind his desk and walked around to sit in one of the two remaining chairs at the coffee table.

"We've been tracking Brett Mara regarding the murder of his wife." *Slow down. This is Harper. No reason to be intimidated.*

"The woman killed in Havana?"

"That's right," Nigel said.

Harper glared at the younger detective, then turned back to Lane. "Why are we investigating a Cuban crime?"

Lane took a breath. "Because we think Brett is back in town. Our investigation is uncovering claims he has been killing seniors. He runs a scam to get them to dip into their savings, then kills them to erase his trail. It also appears that he may be connected with Bill Rogerson."

Harper sat back. "The solicitor general and minister of public security?"

Nigel said, "Kind of ironic if you think about it."

Harper's face turned red, then his scalp. He looked out the window and took a breath.

Here we go. These two can't stand to be in the same room. I should have come here on my own. Lane looked sideways at Nigel, who tried to smile and failed.

"Are you two up for this?" Harper looked at Lane and then at Nigel.

The question from his former partner startled Lane.

"The shooting was what, six months ago? You were cleared. But you look a bit worse for wear. I need to ask —" Harper held his palms open and there was an apology in his eyes.

"Look. I thought about shooting Cori Pierce in the head while I had her cuffed and the snow was all around. My toes were screaming as they warmed up and she kept whining about how her husband forced her. I figured she might pull a Homolka and make a deal. McTavish pulled up and put her in the other truck and that made the decision for me." Lane looked at Harper and then at Nigel. *They both look stunned.* "I haven't told that to anyone, including the shrink. I still get flashbacks, especially when I do some practice shooting."

Harper looked at the ceiling. "I just came from a meeting. Cori Pierce's trial starts next week. Donna Chiu will be testifying. I ran into her. She says her boys are back to normal. The older one is playing his guitar and the younger one is into hockey. She wanted me to say hello and thanks to the pair of you."

"She's a tough one," Nigel said.

"She's a mother who appreciates what you did for her kids." Harper stared right at Lane.

"Can we get this fucking Mara guy off the street before he kills someone else?" Lane asked.

Harper smiled. "So I guess you are doing okay." He turned to Nigel and asked, "Have you got his back? Cori Pierce should never have been allowed to leave Donna's house. I wanna know that it won't happen again." He pointed at Lane without taking his eyes from Nigel. "He got me out after I was shot on some crazy asshole's front step. My partner at the time hid behind the blue and white waiting for backup while I was bleeding. The shooter was on the other side of the door with his rifle. Lane walked up, dressed my wound and got me the hell out of there. I wanna know that you've got his back because it's a safe bet this case will get nasty."

Nigel nodded and looked at the floor.

"The reason you're still here is because Lane vouched for you. He says you did what you were trained to do. You hear me?"

Nigel nodded.

Enough of this! Lane thought. "Back off, Cam. Nigel did exactly what needed to be done in that situation. I trust him. There was no collateral damage. Now, can we work on getting this guy off the street, please?"

Harper nodded. "Okay. I'll see what I can find out about Rogerson."

Lane got up and shook Harper's hand. *There was the briefest of smiles on his face. He was playing me!*

"You understand I had to ask." Harper looked Lane in the eye.

Lane smiled and nodded.

When they reached their car parked on the street, Nigel asked, "Why did you smile and shake his hand?"

Lane opened the passenger door and got in. He waited for Nigel to get behind the wheel, then said, "He was doing his job, seeing if you and I were still on our game. If this case means we are going after the solicitor general, then Harper will be in it up to his eyebrows. He was making sure we are okay after the shooting. He knows what it's like because it took him a while to recover after he was wounded. Now, we need to see Fibre." Fibre — more formally Dr. Colin Weaver — was head of the Forensic Crime Scene Unit. Lane pulled his phone out of his pocket and began to dial the doctor's number.

"Thank you." Nigel put on his seat belt and started the car.

"I explained already. You didn't fire because you weren't supposed to. You followed your training. Harper wasn't there. You and I were. We did what had to be done." Lane leaned back and closed his eyes. He was struck by a flashback of the bullet hitting Pierce's eye and his body falling. The blood on the floor. Two boys screaming. The stink of urine. Lane opened his eyes. "We need to get some Crave Cupcakes."

"For Fibre?"

Lane nodded.

"I thought he liked Nanaimo bars." Nigel looked over his shoulder and backed up.

"We have two favours to ask this time." Lane looked down the road as traffic collected at a red light. "We need to sweeten the deal."

Nigel shoulder checked and pulled out. "Kensington and then Foothills?"

Lane nodded.

"You're gonna give the guy type-two diabetes." Dr. Weaver had the physique of a male model.

Lane smiled. "Everyone needs at least one guilty pleasure."

"So we're stopping for a coffee at the same time?"

"That's right. We've got some thinking to do."

After picking up a dozen Crave Cupcakes, they stopped for lunch at Kienna in Kensington. They sat just inside the door and near the window. Lane had a croissant and Nigel had a sandwich. Lane finished about half the croissant and waited until he saw that Nigel had a mouthful of food. He said, "When I was six or seven, the girl next door had a baby. I used to hear the baby crying when I was in my room. One night I even saw the baby with its mother. She was young, maybe fifteen or sixteen."

Nigel nodded, chewed and watched his partner.

A two-year-old girl in pink shorts and a purple top pounded across the wood floor followed by her white-bearded grandfather. Lane smiled at the scene. "A couple of months later, I saw her brothers digging a hole in the back garden. I asked my mother about it and she took a belt to me. The rest of that summer there was a smell in the air — especially after their dog dug a hole back there. I didn't recognize the smell until my first murder investigation. Anyway, I ran into the baby's mother in Cuba and she asked if I could help give the baby a proper burial. I agreed to help."

Nigel wiped his lips with a napkin. "That's the second thing you need to ask Fibre?"

Lane nodded and took another bite of croissant.

"Okay. I'm in."

They met Fibre twenty minutes later in his antiseptic office where three framed drawings hung on the right-hand wall: one piece of original art by each of his triplets. Fibre sat behind his glass-topped desk, perfectly groomed with manicured hands atop a sheet of paper as if the nails were set out to dry. *Parenthood certainly appears to agree with him. He's still got a full head of blond hair.* Lane glanced at the photographs of the triplets. *And each one has his blue eyes.*

Nigel set the dozen assorted cupcakes on the nearest edge of the desk.

Fibre leaned forward and pulled the cupcakes to his side of the desk. He looked at Lane. "How are you feeling?"

I can't remember him asking me a question like that before. "I'm okay."

"That's not really an answer." The doctor undid the ribbon wrapped around the clear plastic cupcake container.

Just give it to him straight up. "I'm learning to live with being a killer. On a logical level I understand that I did what needed to be done to protect a family and myself. On an emotional level I sometimes wonder what separates me from the people I hunt."

Nigel remained uncharacteristically silent. Fibre lifted his head. "Which is the predominant response, logic or emotion?"

Lane shrugged. "Depends on the day."

Fibre picked out an angel food cupcake with strawberry icing and popped it in his mouth. He chewed, studied the detectives, reached for a tissue, spat the paper cupcake wrapper into it, rolled the tissue into a ball, leaned over and dropped it in the garbage.

Don't smile! And for damn sure, don't laugh, Lane thought. He felt a giggle tickling him somewhere near his lowest rib. He coughed into his hand. "We have a suspect who may be preying on the elderly in seniors residences. Would you be willing to look at some deaths to see whether they may have been misdiagnosed as myocardial infarctions?"

Fibre picked up a chocolate cupcake with chocolate icing. This time, he carefully peeled off the paper cup before popping the delicacy in his mouth. He covered his mouth with his right hand. "Yes."

"Nigel will be your contact?" Lane took a deep breath. *Hang on! Don't laugh!*

Fibre closed his eyes and nodded.

Hurry up! "Also, I'd like you to look into a cold case. I believe we know where the body of an infant is buried in a backyard. I was hoping you would help with the exhumation. The mother is requesting a proper burial."

Fibre opened his eyes and took a long look at the drawings on the wall. He reached to pick up and unwrap another chocolate cupcake. He closed the container with his free hand and popped the treat in his mouth with the other, then looked at Lane. "Get me the specifics and as accurate a location as possible. How many years have passed?"

"Nearly forty," Lane said.

Fibre chewed, then licked his fingers, opened a drawer and pulled out a wet wipe. He carefully cleaned each finger. "We may need some ground radar."

"Thank you." Lane stood up but did not offer his hand until Fibre did. They shook. "How are the kids?"

Fibre beamed. "Beautiful." He tapped the box of cupcakes. "Crave Cupcakes are their favourite."

Lane followed Nigel out of the office and onto the elevator. They rode down in silence, did not make eye contact as they walked outside, kept their eyes on the car as they crossed the street and got inside the Chev.

Nigel looked at Lane. "I thought you were going to choke when he spat out the cupcake wrapper."

Lane smiled and began to laugh. *It's been a while since I've been able to do that.*

Nigel started the engine. "Where to?"

"Where's Carlo right now?"

Nigel pulled out his phone, tapped it a couple of times, checked the Street Food app, then said, "We might just make it. He's over by Deerfoot."

Fifteen minutes later, they spotted Carlo's Calzones parked in a line of food trucks east of a warehouse and behind a couple of metal shipping containers. Carlo was lowering the awning. He turned as they parked next to one of the containers and got out of the Chev. The pink Fries and Dolls food truck beeped its horn as it drove away. Carlo waved, then turned to Lane. "What's up?"

Lane said, "A couple of things."

Carlo walked to the front of the truck and leaned on the glacial-blue fender.

Lane moved to within a metre of the man who smelled of cheese, tomato sauce and cooking oil. Carlo smiled. "I know, I smell like a calzone."

Nigel laughed.

"I want you to check our list of seniors residences. I want to see which ones you're sure he's worked at already. That way we can shorten our list." Lane looked over his shoulder at Nigel, who had his handheld computer out so that Carlo could read the screen.

Carlo leaned over to see the list, then lifted his chin at Lane. "Were you the cop who shot that university prof who was going to kill that family?"

Lane nodded. *Where's he going with this?* "That's correct."

"The trial of his wife begins next week." Carlo studied Lane.

"Again, correct."

Carlo looked at Nigel's list, back at Lane, then at the graffiti on the container. He took about ten seconds, then asked, "Will this be a two-way sharing of information?" His finger pointed at the detectives, then at his own chest.

Lane shook his head. "Probably not. But I will let you know when we have him in custody."

Carlo pulled his phone out of his pocket. "What's your phone number and e-mail?"

Lane told him and he entered the information.

Carlo continued. "I checked on some of the other information. I don't know what Brett and his buddy have on the politician, but the word is that he's the FKs' puppet. It's kind of funny when you think about it: the guy in charge of law and order is working for a gang."

Nigel didn't smile. "Fuckin' hilarious."

Lane asked, "Can I borrow your phone?"

Carlo shook his head. "No."

"Then show me while you put my cell number on your favourites. And I want your assurance you will call me first whenever you get more information." Lane took a half step closer to Carlo, who stopped leaning and glared at the officer. "Your grandmother looked after you and now I'm looking after you. That's the way you need to see this. I don't want you to get into trouble by taking care of this on your own."

Carlo smiled and pulled his phone out of his pocket. "What is your number again?" He entered Lane's phone number, then turned to Nigel. "Let's see that list."

✕

Walter felt his body humming with anxiety as he watched the blonde-haired woman of about forty set up the pen for the rabbits. She prepared the square course once a week to give the rabbit pair some exercise and to provide some entertainment for residents and guests. Walter had had Penny dress him in his best tan sweatpants and a white shirt. He smiled when he spotted the two children entering the south entrance of the atrium. The boy, dressed in blue shorts, red T-shirt and a blue ball cap, stopped to watch the rabbits. His blonde sister wore pink shorts, a pink top and pink shoes. She bounced as she ran and headed for the bench, pulled herself up and began to swing. Stacey, her mother, rushed over before the bench and the toddler ended up in the foliage. Another family arrived. The granddaughter was about six years old and carried a grey stuffed rabbit. She leaned over the enclosure and squeezed the grey rabbit. It announced, "I'm Thumper!"

Staff member Laura walked past with Shauday. They both wore purple tops and pants with white running shoes. Today they wore their black hair long. It reached past their shoulder blades. Walter smiled at the pair. They smiled back, then walked past to sit under a palm tree where they could eat lunch and chat.

Walter turned back to watch Stacey set the toddler on her feet. Stacey looked to be about thirty, had long black hair with a streak of grey and wore black pants and a blue top. She went over and sat next to Cora, whose hair was tightly curled and silver white. Her husband had died last year, and her granddaughter brought the great-grandkids out on "rabbit days."

Walter couldn't hear what they were saying even though he had his hearing aids in. He watched intently and cursed that he'd forgotten to ask Penny to clean his glasses. The toddler climbed up into her mother's lap as the boy leaned in close to watch the rabbits hop their obstacle course.

Walter looked left and saw Brett watching Cora, Stacey and the kids. There was a smile on his lips as he leaned against the wall and stacked the heel of one clog atop the toe of the other. The kindness of Brett's round, welcoming face was betrayed by the dark predatory green in his eyes.

Cora began to breathe quickly. Her eyes closed and she slumped forward. Stacey reached out and caught her before she could fall to the cement. "Help me!" Walter saw the fear in Brett's eyes when he stood up straight, then launched himself forward. He took Cora and set her down on the ground on her back. Stacey watched with her daughter as Brett began CPR.

Soon Laura and Shauday were there. One put a cushion under Cora's head. The old woman's eyes blinked open. Walter could see her face looking up from between Laura's white shoes. He read Cora's lips when she asked, "Am I in hell?"

×

Lane had his sports jacket over his shoulder as he finished the forty-minute walk home from the LRT station. The sun was low in the sky yet he could still feel the heat of the day radiating up through the soles of his feet. He looked ahead at his house where mugo pines grew underneath the dining room windows. The street was unusually empty of vehicles. *Looks like no one's home.*

Lane went up the steps and saw Sam watching him through the living room window. It was open and he could hear the dog's tail slapping against the back of the leather chair. Lane smiled as he opened the door. *The dog is always glad to see me.*

He looked down and saw there were no shoes at the front door. He kicked off his shoes, then scratched Sam behind the ear. "How's my boy?"

He hung his jacket in the closet and walked into the kitchen, right into a crowd of family and friends. "What the hell?"

Christine held Indiana on her hip and said. "You had no idea, did you, detective?"

"It's your birthday!" Arthur said.

Lane felt his mouth fall open. *It is! Christ, I forgot!*

Matt said, "We all chipped in and got you this." They stepped aside to expose a pair of boxes wrapped in silver paper.

"What is it?" Lane asked.

Dan said, "We're all waiting for a cup."

"You forgot, didn't you?" Arthur had one hand on his hip and pointed a finger with the other.

Lane blushed as he reached for Indiana, who tucked his head next to Lane's neck. "How are you today?"

Matt said, "We decided on a small party. I hope that's okay."

Lane nodded. "Small is better."

Christine lifted one of the boxes onto the kitchen table. "Hurry up. We want to see what you think."

Lane settled Indiana onto his right hip and tore at the silver wrapping paper with his left hand. Underneath the paper were the words *Rancillio* and *espresso*. He looked around at the expectant faces. "How did you know I've wanted one of these?"

Christine rolled her eyes. Arthur looked sideways at his partner and crossed his arms. Matt laughed out loud. Dan shook his head and asked, "You're kidding, right?"

Lane moved to the second package, pulled at the wrapping and saw that it contained a coffee grinder. Matt pulled the grinder out of its package and Dan did the same with the shiny new espresso machine. Within five minutes they had both machines set up and sitting on the blue pearl granite counter.

Arthur said, "Come on, we've got a reservation for dinner."

They travelled downtown in two vehicles and parked out front of Lane's favourite Italian restaurant. Lane remembered Nina, the owner's daughter. She had been terrifically shy around almost everyone through junior high, but began to talk to Lane in grade ten. He remembered the taste of the ham and pineapple pizza Nina's mother used to make and the Orange Crush he would always drink with his food.

Arthur parked in front of Pulcinella and waited for the kids to arrive. Sam, the manager, wore a white shirt, black slacks, close-trimmed black hair and a five o'clock shadow on a round face. He smiled and asked, "Reservation?"

"Merali for five and a baby."

Sam handed the menus to his female assistant and turned to Lane, saying, "Good to see you again." Christine led the way with Indiana in the crook of one arm. Dan followed with a bag overflowing with baby necessities. They sat down under the sign explaining the history of Toto, the clown prince of Naples, ordered drinks and checked over the menu. Lane took Indiana for a look at the oven and the chefs making pizza. They could see the wood glowing orange and yellow at the back of the oven. The chef used a long-handed paddle to rotate pizzas, then remove them. Indiana pointed to the chef on the right, who wore a white jacket and hat. He sliced portions of dough and set them on the granite. Lane moved over to allow Indiana a closer look as the dough was flattened, then launched into the air and twirled by the chef's fists.

"How are you?"

Lane looked to his right and saw a woman who looked to be about his age. She stood a head shorter than he. Her shoulder-length hair was black, her skin tanned. Her red blouse and black skirt looked to be tailor made. "Nina?"

The woman smiled. "You remembered. And who is this?"

Some women gather up beauty bit by bit as they get older, and you are one of them. "His name is Indiana. The son of my niece." He lifted his chin to point at the table where his family was focused on conversation.

"Nina!" Nina and Lane turned to see who had waved at her from the kitchen.

Nina touched Lane's arm and said, "My brother. You remember Fernando?"

Lane blushed. *Of course I remember him! I had a huge crush on him.* He watched as Fernando shook his head, then disappeared behind the oven to reappear in the hallway leading to the washrooms. He was about twenty pounds heavier than when Lane had last seen him, his black hair was streaked with grey, but his chin still had that cleft in it. His brown eyes were black with rage, however. He waved for Nina to follow him. She touched Lane's elbow and said, "Excuse me," then went down the hallway.

Lane turned and spotted Christine, who waved him over. Lane held Indiana close to him and sat down across from Christine. He saw a man in a suit and a woman in a white outfit sitting at the table next to his niece. He recognized the professional way they scanned the room and the patrons. The pair kept looking toward the couple sitting next to the wall on the other side of the restaurant. Christine held out her arms. He lifted Indiana and handed the boy across the table to his mother. Lane glanced over his shoulder and saw a woman with short brown hair sitting with her back to him, and a girl of twelve or thirteen with shoulder-length red hair. He turned back and saw the man in the suit and the woman in white studying him. He nodded. They made no acknowledgement. Lane took another quick look and realized it was the premier having dinner with her daughter. The pair at the next table were her bodyguards.

The waitress arrived. She looked to be in her mid twenties, wore a black top and skirt, and appeared to be nine months pregnant. Christine asked, "Do you know what it is?"

The waitress smiled, nodded and said, "Girl." She tapped her belly. "Four weeks to go."

As she took their orders, Arthur asked, "Are you feeling all right?"

"Really good. No morning sickness. Must have been because of all the times before when I drank too much." She covered her mouth.

Christine laughed. "Okay if I have the Romano?" The orders came quickly after that.

"Won't be long." The waitress wrote down their orders and left.

"Who was that woman who came up to you?" Arthur asked.

Lane realized everyone at the table was interested in the answer. "Nina. I went to high school with her. We were friends. Her family used to own this place years ago when it was a pizza restaurant. I think her brother owns this place now, and she owns another one in Bridgeland."

Dan looked over Lane's shoulder. *He's going to figure it out any second now.*

Matt looked in the other direction where four women in their twenties sat together. Each was long legged. Three were blonde. All wore clothing that was too expensive to have come off the rack from The Bay. And all were stunning. Then Matt looked left where two beautiful dark-haired women faced him. *I wonder if he'll be able to eat his dinner?*

A hand tapped Lane on the shoulder and he turned to see Nina, who looked at Arthur when she asked, "Would you mind if I borrowed him for a few minutes?" She offered her hand and Arthur took it.

Arthur shook her hand. "It's his birthday."

Nina looked at Lane. "Is it?"

Christine said, "This is his favourite restaurant."

Nina turned to Lane. "Do you have a minute?"

Lane nodded and got up. The spines of the premier's security guards straightened. They watched Nina and Lane as he followed her back along the hallway to the bathroom and out the back door. She opened the door and held it for him as they stepped into the back alley where cars and garbage containers vied for limited space. A black Escalade sat in the middle of the alley. Fernando stood at the open passenger door. Lane spotted the driver, who appeared to be over six feet tall and to weigh more than two hundred and fifty pounds. *What did they call it in high school? Was it pasta power?* "What's up?" Lane asked. Fernando reached out and shook the detective's hand. Lane felt himself blushing and was glad the sun was low and the shadows were deepening.

Fernando pointed at the back seat of the Escalade. Lane moved closer to the open passenger door, leaned in the cab and spotted the wide eyes of a man with duct tape over his mouth. Another strip of tape went around his forehead and held him to the rear headrest. The prisoner wore a black suit and blue tie, and his hands were wrapped with more duct tape. The shoulder belt held him where he sat. Lane turned to Fernando and Nina. "What's going on?"

Fernando said, "This guy has been ripping off some of the old people in our neighbourhood. He charms some lonely old lady, then tells her he works at her bank. That he needs her to transfer twenty-five thousand dollars to catch the thief who works there. He already ripped off Angelo's mom. This afternoon he showed up at my mom's place. I dropped by just after he arrived. I called Angelo and we tried to get his mother's money back. But..." Fernando shrugged.

"Why did you bring him here and not to the police?" Lane asked.

"I wanted to ask my sister's advice." Fernando looked at the ground.

Nina rolled her eyes. "I insisted that we ask you what to do next."

"You have a lawyer?" Lane asked.

Nina nodded.

"Any good?" Lane looked at Fernando, who looked sideways at Angelo.

Nina said, "Yes, she's our cousin."

Lane said, "Good. Call the lawyer and have her meet you at the downtown office on 6th Avenue. Wait for your lawyer, then take the suspect in and explain that you made a citizen's arrest. That you have witnesses who will back up your story about the frauds. Explain how this suspect has been scamming seniors."

Nina asked, "Should we call the media?"

Lane shook his head. "See how things go first. Media is a wild card."

Nina pulled out her phone, dialed and spoke. "Carla. We need your help right away. Can you meet Fernando at the downtown police station on sixth? Fernando will explain." She handed the phone to her brother, took Lane's elbow and led the way back to the door. "Thanks for the help. Fernando was pretty pissed. Since my dad died, Fernando has been more protective of Mom. He needed to cool down and think of other options."

His first option probably involved a shovel and a drive to the country. "No problem." They went back inside, where Lane sat down and Nina went to talk with the waitress.

"What was that about?" Arthur asked.

"Some family business. They needed a little advice." Lane saw a waiter approaching with pizzas in each hand. Christine's came first, then Matt's. Another waiter brought Arthur's pizza piled high with fresh arugula and prosciutto.

Lane's arrived moments later. The mix of anchovies, mozza-rella, tomato sauce and basil smelled heavenly. There wasn't much talk for the next few minutes. Indiana drank a bottle of formula while he sat with Dan, who ate with his right hand while Christine cut his pizza into sections.

Motion caught Lane's eye. The bodyguards stood up. The detective looked right. The premier was standing and waiting for her daughter to follow. The premier turned and made eye contact with Lane. He saw an instant of surprise in her eyes before she nodded and said, "Detective."

How does she know me? he thought. Then he smiled when he recalled what had gone on in the back alley. The premier's bodyguards had no idea. He watched their backs as they left the restaurant.

chapter 12

Marvin died sometime in the early morning. Walter woke up a little after nine. The nurse had come in to change Marvin's pain patch. Instead, she found a corpse. There was a flurry of people in and out. Walter saw that Marvin's new patch had been left on the table between their beds. He looked at it for quite some time. They brought a gurney in, loaded up Marvin's body and eased him out the door. Walter leaned over, gripped the package with his thumb and forefinger and stuffed it between the buttons of his pajama top.

Lane and Nigel sat behind the forty-two-inch screen on Lane's desk and made sure all the bits of the investigation were on the map. "What about this?" Nigel asked. He pointed at the green box with the name of the solicitor general.

Lane leaned back in his chair and thought about the fact that the premier knew who he was and what it might mean. *We're trying to catch Mara before he kills again. If Rogerson can get us closer to that, then we need to see the solicitor general.* "I'll call Rogerson."

Lori looked up the number and called the solicitor general's office. It took twenty minutes of being on hold and speaking with a trio of assistants before she transferred the call to Lane. "Detective Lane with the Calgary Police Service. I need to meet with Mr. Rogerson."

"Might I enquire about the nature of your business?"

Business? Lane thought. "It regards a murder investigation."

"The solicitor general would like to help in any way possible, of course."

"But?"

"You must understand he is very busy."

Up goes the stonewall. Let's see how this does against the wall. "There have been allegations of organized crime involvement."

"As part of the murder investigation?"

"That is correct."

"Could I have your contact information? I will get back to you within fifteen minutes."

Lane gave the information, hung up his phone and looked at the time. He set the stopwatch on his phone, then looked at Nigel and asked, "Can you find out where Rogerson is today? He's a Calgary MLA."

Nigel nodded, got up and rolled his chair over to his computer.

Lori said, "I'll see what I can find out."

Lane's cell phone rang four minutes later. "Lane here."

"It's Cam. Did you try to set up a meet with the solicitor general?"

"Yes. I made the call four minutes ago."

"You alleged he was involved with organized crime?"

"I was being stonewalled and mentioned allegations of organized crime. In no way did I suggest that Rogerson was or is connected with organized crime, although that is the allegation from a reliable source." Lane looked at Nigel, who looked over his shoulder and raised his eyebrows.

"What made you decide to go after Rogerson?"

"Went out for dinner last night. The premier was there. She recognized me."

"You've met her before?" Harper asked.

"No."

It took Harper about fifteen seconds to process the new information. "Keep me in the loop and keep digging."

"Will do."

Harper hung up.

Nigel said, "That was quick."

"Very. Apparently we are going to be under some very well-connected scrutiny for the remainder of this case." Lane looked at the map on his screen and typed the date and time of the conversations with Rogerson's representative and Harper.

"Either they're afraid of the whiff of a scandal, or there is a scandal and they're afraid we're going to sniff it out." Nigel looked at his screen and frowned.

Lori poked her head in the door. "Rogerson will be at Mewata Armoury in twenty minutes."

Lane stood up and looked at the stopwatch on his phone. They were up to twelve minutes. He looked at it again when it read twenty-seven minutes. Rogerson's handler still hadn't returned the call when Nigel parked the Chevy across the street from Mewata. The armoury was red brick and sandstone with a couple of turrets out front of the sloped red roof. A Sherman tank was parked to the left-hand side of the main door, which looked like a castle gate. "This has to be the oddest, most medieval-looking building in the city," Nigel said as he removed the keys and got out of the car.

Lane got out the other side and closed the door. "Built in 1917 and it looks older." He looked around at the condominiums, LRT bridge, shops, office buildings and vehicle dealerships all within one hundred metres. *It's an anachronism.* They walked to the crosswalk, then looked to see whether any traffic was approaching and crossed the street.

"Sometimes you're so prim and proper." Nigel walked beside him.

"You mean because I use the crosswalk?"

"That and other things." Nigel looked at Lane's shoes and then his tie.

Lane shrugged as they walked up to the front door of the armoury and inside to an open area with white walls and white stripes painted on the floor. In the corner he spotted a camera light, a TV crew and a knot of reservists. They wore green fatigues and flanked the solicitor general. His voice carried in the echo–chamber emptiness of the cavernous area, which often served as a parade ground. "In my role as solicitor general and minster of public security, it is an honour to be here today to recognize these Albertans and their service to our community."

He has a very convincing voice. And he is really good at playing to the audience.

"Our reservists volunteer their time and effort to serve our country, some of them overseas." Rogerson took a step forward while facing the cameras. "They are the pride of this province. Today we honour five outstanding members."

Nigel followed Lane as they walked in behind the cameras and into Rogerson's line of sight. The solicitor general's hair was cut high and tight. His face was round and his neck was a straight line from ears to shoulders. He wore a tailored white shirt and grey suit set off by a red tie and a Canadian flag pinned to his lapel. He glanced at the detectives, then away as he introduced the reservists and presented them with stars. "All five served overseas," Rogerson began, then spoke for twenty more minutes about each reservist's contributions. He shook the hand of each man, and then the camera lights turned off. "Thank you and goodbye," he said, and his smile died.

Lane waited with his hands at his sides. As the solicitor general began to move, Lane executed an angle to intercept. When he was within two metres, he said, "We need a moment, Mr. Rogerson."

Rogerson lifted his chin and smiled. "Follow me."

Lane walked alongside the politician. Nigel took the other side, and they walked out the front door to stop next to the

Sherman tank. Someone had painted a white peace symbol on its grey turret.

Lane held up his identification. Rogerson crossed his arms and looked at the detective. "What can I do for you?"

"Do you know Brett Mara?" Lane asked.

"I went to high school with a Brett Mara." Rogerson turned on the smile.

The smile means nothing. Get right to the point. "Did Mara or one of his associates ask you to initiate a private member's bill to allow private companies like MCSC to operate seniors residences in the province?"

"I brought in the bill because seniors in the province need safe and secure places to live out their twilight years." Rogerson put his hands in his pockets and leaned back on his heels.

Nigel asked, "How much did MCSC contribute to your party?"

Rogerson said, "You tell me. I think you already know the answer to that question."

Lane tapped the side of the tank. *Get him looking this way so he feels like the questions are coming from all sides.* "Do you know the current whereabouts of Brett Mara?"

Rogerson shook his head. "No."

Lane said, "We'll be in touch."

"In the meantime I want you to do something about this." Rogerson pointed at the peace symbol on the tank.

"We'll get right on it," Nigel said.

Lane turned and walked to the crosswalk.

Nigel stood next to him as a city bus rumbled by. "He was playing with us, wasn't he?"

Lane nodded. "That he was, the arrogant bastard." They crossed the street. When they reached the other side Lane said, "It's beginning to feel like we're pawns in somebody's game. I need to have a private conversation with Cam."

They met at the Lucky Elephant Restaurant in Chinatown. Lane wore his grey jacket and blue pants. Harper wore a blue golf shirt and black pants.

The waiter wore a black short-sleeved shirt and pants. A gold elephant hung on a chain around his neck. There were dragon tattoos on both of his arms. "Can I take your order?"

"Number forty, please?" Lane closed his menu and handed it to the waiter.

"Thirty-five." Harper handed his menu over and reached for his beer.

"Uncle Tran here today?" Lane asked.

The waiter smiled and shook his head. "He took the week off to go trail riding in the foothills." He turned and walked through the swinging saloon doors and into the kitchen.

Lane looked around. A couple sat at the other end of the restaurant. The supper rush had come and gone.

Harper put his beer down and looked at his watch. "What's up?"

"It looks like there's a leak. I ran into the premier at a restaurant the other day and she recognized me. We interviewed the solicitor general today and he was ready for us." Lane took a sip of tea, then refilled his cup.

Harper nodded and looked at the ceiling. "There is something going on. But I haven't got a handle on it yet. I mentioned our conversation to Simpson and no one else."

"What about Rogerson?" Lane glanced at the jade elephant near the cash register and smiled as he recalled its secret.

Harper shook his head. "No idea. Unless of course he is in contact with Brett Mara and the other so-called investors who want to bring Mi Casa Su Casa into the province."

"Nigel's done some research and discovered that private companies like MCSC have been major contributors to the ruling party."

"Doesn't surprise me, and it's probably all legal."

Lane raised his eyebrows.

"I know, it stinks." Harper leaned back as his bowl of noodles topped with chicken and egg rolls arrived. "But it's legal."

Lane's satay beef noodle soup arrived and he inhaled the sharp sweet scents of satay, green onions, coconut milk and chili peppers. He grabbed his chopsticks and picked up a slice of beef and some noodles.

Harper picked at his food. "Lately, all the actions I should be taking seem to take a back seat to politics."

Lane leaned on his elbows. "How are the kids?"

"Growing like crazy. When I get home, I'm just Dad." Harper smiled. "How is your brood? I've been wondering what Indiana will call you." He picked up a slice of chicken with his chopsticks and popped it in his mouth.

"He'll come up with something." Lane picked up the spoon and scooped up some broth.

"Maybe he'll call you Lane as well."

Lane shrugged as he savoured the spices in the broth. "He gives great hugs and he doesn't throw up as much as he used to."

"More fun is yet to come." Harper pointed his chopsticks at his old partner. "I'll find out what I can from my end. The leak has me worried. I'd really like to plug that first."

Lane nodded. "Lori knows all of the secretaries. I'll check with her and see what she can find out. They usually know more about what's going on than anyone else."

✕

Walter pressed the button on the slot machine. He sat next to his daughter, who turned to smile at him. Her black hair was greying. Her brown eyes were bright. She nudged him with her elbow.

He turned back to his machine just in time to see the last bar fall into line. His arms shot up in the air and he almost fell off his stool. Linda's hand was on his shoulder and it steadied him. "Cash out, Dad."

Walter pressed another button and a piece of paper rolled out of an opening. "Five thousand. We won five thousand dollars!"

He opened his eyes and looked around the room. The empty bed beside him. The flat-screen TV in front. The pictures of Linda and his wife on the table next to the bed. He looked down at his hand and the permanent purple-bruised colour of its flesh. There was no slip of paper between his fingers. What was worse was remembering that Linda was gone — dead for more than a year.

chapter 13

Lane woke up to the sun shining along the vertical gap in the burgundy curtains of their bedroom. He looked at the clock. It was after nine and he could hear activity in the kitchen. Coffee sputtered from the espresso machine. Indiana pounded a fist on the table of his high chair. A dish clattered and the dishwasher door shut.

"Indiana!" Christine said.

Lane looked up at the ceiling, threw back the covers and headed for the bathroom.

Fifteen minutes later he went downstairs wearing a T-shirt and shorts.

Indiana smiled despite wearing puréed carrots on his cheeks and chin and in his eyebrows. Christine wore a white top and red fleece pajama bottoms. She snuck up on her son with a washcloth. His head twisted from side to side as he attempted to avoid the clean-up.

"Where is everyone?" Lane asked.

Christine grabbed the catches on either side of the high chair, pulled the table away, undid the seat belt and lifted Indiana out. "Arthur went shopping. Matt and Dan are at work. Want a coffee?"

Lane lifted his eyebrows and reached for Indiana.

Christine smiled. "I know, stupid question." She turned to the espresso machine, reached for the portafilter, turned on the coffee grinder, filled the basket, then locked it in place. Steam erupted, milk was heated until it frothed, coffee spluttered and the ingredients were carefully mixed. One cup was handed to Lane. Christine sipped from the other. She'd left a leaf design on top of his latte. "How about we go for a walk after I get him ready?"

"Okay." *This is perfect. I love having one of these at home.* Lane sipped his coffee and popped a couple of slices of bread into the toaster. Twenty minutes later they had Sam on a leash, Indy in the stroller and the sun on their faces. They walked down the paved pathway across the street from the separate school where a sign announced that non-Catholics could inquire about registering. Indy's eyelids began to droop as Sam tugged at the leash. It was tied to the handle of the three-wheeled stroller. The leaves of mature poplar trees shaded the pathway and the temperature hovered around twenty-five.

A tan-and-white boxer approached. It stared down Sam, who began to jump and howl. The boxer hit the end of its leash and began to bark. Christine grabbed Sam's leash, then rolled him on his back and held her hand on his chest until he calmed. The boxer's owner tapped his walking stick on the concrete as he passed without saying a word or making eye contact. Sam stopped wriggling and whimpering after the man and his boxer disappeared around a corner. "You done?" Christine asked Sam as she let him up. He shook the dust off his back and sat.

"Where did you learn that trick?" Lane leaned over to see how Indy was doing. The baby had the end of a nylon strap in his mouth. There was drool on his chin.

"Paradise. One of the women there really knew how to handle dogs and she showed me how to grab a leg and roll them on their backs to calm things down." She walked ahead. Sam began to pull. Christine tugged the leash sideways and he slowed. "How are you doing?"

Lane shrugged. "All right."

"Everyone keeps asking how you are after what happened with Pierce. I don't know what to tell them." Christine looked at her uncle and waited.

She asked so just tell her the truth. "More and more I'm beginning to understand that I did my job. For the first few weeks I kept thinking about what I could have done to prevent what happened, but—" he saw she was holding her lips tight, and he shook his head "— I dealt with what was in front of me. He was going to shoot one of the boys and he had to be stopped."

"Matt says he shot at you first and missed."

Lane nodded and shrugged. "He got one shot off and it hit the wall next to me. The next three shots were from my weapon."

"Three?"

"Even after being shot, a person can keep going if there's enough adrenalin in his system." He shuddered with a flashback. Pierce lifted his gun. Lane put a round in the professor's eye, life left the body and it collapsed.

"Sorry. You just turned white."

Lane took a long slow breath. "It's okay. I don't mind talking with you. You listen. There are still flashbacks. Now they come less frequently."

Christine waited for him to say more as they took another half dozen steps forward.

Lane said, "Part of my problem was how easy it was to take a life. For a while I wondered what made me any different from the people I hunt down. Then there was this nagging doubt about how I might react if a similar situation came along."

"React?"

"It might be easier if there's a next time. That worries me."

"Or more difficult. What else?"

Lane looked at his niece thoughtfully. *When did our roles reverse? How long have you been taking care of me? Maybe now we just take care of each other.* "When I know what it is that's bothering me, I'll tell you, okay? Right now I'm not exactly sure what it is."

×

Walter sat next to the birdcage in the atrium and watched the expressions on the faces of people walking by. Laura and Shauday walked by with lunches in hand. They wore peach tops and bottoms today. Both still had black hair extensions. They looked left at the birds. *They must be pretty loud today. Glad I can't hear the noisy buggers.* Walter looked at the budgies and watched their beaks.

Brett and his spring-loaded clogs passed by. Walter used the palm of his left hand to push the tire of his left wheel. He finally managed to swing the chair so he could see Brett approach Cora, who smiled in recognition. She sat in one of the green wingback chairs. *That's one good thing about the wheelchair,* Walter thought. *With all of the incontinence — what's wrong with saying* shit *and* piss *anyway? — going on around here, sitting in one of those fabric-covered chairs is never a good idea.*

Brett grabbed a nearby rattan chair by the arms and moved it so he sat across from Cora. He reached into the pocket of his shirt and pulled out a piece of paper. Walter watched Cora's smile fade to be replaced by wide-eyed horror. She mimicked Brett when he mimed zipping his lips. Brett folded the paper and put it back in his pocket. He leaned forward and took Cora's hands. She nodded as he spoke. Then Brett got up, nodded at her and walked away. Cora put her hands in her lap and looked at Walter without seeing him.

Walter tapped his belly with the palm of his right hand and felt the plastic wrapped patch under his shirt and wondered if one fentanyl patch would be strong enough to finish Brett.

×

Anna wore a fitted red T-shirt with black slacks and had her blonde hair tied at the back. Nigel had first met her at high school. Now they were dating. She was also Nigel's go-to cyber source. She sat across from Nigel, who wore a mauve shirt and grey shorts, beside the window of the Holy Grill, a restaurant across the street from Mountain Equipment Co-op. They were just south of downtown and its gold-and-blue towers.

It was after one and the lunch crowd had thinned. All three nearby tables were empty.

Anna leaned closer. "I did some checking into Mi Casa Su Casa. Just nibbling around the edges. Nothing serious."

Nigel frowned and looked around to see if anyone was listening in. A couple with a toddler was busy trying to feed a moving target. A retired couple sat across from each other. He read the paper; she read the front page. Nigel said, "I was told not to involve you."

"I was very careful. Their financial statements to shareholders just do not add up. I used their own numbers and it looks like they are making them up. They must be operating some kind of Ponzi scheme because the money they're paying back to shareholders is not sustainable. It looks like the CEO is trying to hook new investors with promises of returns in the neighbourhood of twenty percent. I looked into the CEO's investments, and she just purchased a property in the Caymans." Anna leaned back, waiting for Nigel's reaction.

He nodded. "No extradition treaty."

"One of the guys who scammed gold investors in Calgary still lives in the Caymans."

"Nigel!" The chef behind the chrome-and-glass counter set up three plates.

Anna got up and Nigel followed. They returned with a blackened chicken burger for her, Thai chicken soup for him and a bowl of fries to share.

Anna took a bite of her burger and waited for Nigel to try his soup before covering her mouth. She said, "You've been really quiet this last month. What's the problem?"

Nigel savoured the mixture of spices, chicken and squash, then swallowed. "I'm just trying to be a bit less of a big mouth." He smiled. "I'm trying to think before saying something."

"It sounds to me like you're trying to avoid talking about what's really bothering you."

Nigel shrugged. "It's no big deal." He frowned and stared at the opposite wall.

"Then why are you acting so different?"

Nigel put down his spoon. "I don't know."

Anna set her burger down. Her voice dropped to a whisper and she pointed her finger at him. "Bullshit! Let me know what's going on in there!" She pressed her forefinger against his forehead. "You are becoming more and more distant. You were like this after what happened to your mom. It must have been two years before you emerged from that dark place."

Nigel's eyes focused and he made eye contact with her. "I keep having flashbacks of Lane shooting that guy."

Anna leaned back. The blush of anger disappeared from her cheeks and forehead.

"Pierce was going to shoot the kid, and then he shot at Lane. And Lane just aimed and fired twice. Pierce kind of stood there. His gun dropped a bit, then he brought it back up. Lane put a round in Pierce's eye and he collapsed. All of his muscles just turned into jelly. The kids were crying and screaming. I keep seeing and hearing it over and over again." Nigel stared at the oranges and reds in the Thai soup.

"You think Lane was wrong?"

Nigel shook his head. "That's not it at all. I think I froze. Lane says I did what my training taught me. That the mother and father were in my line of fire."

"Were they?"

Nigel nodded. "They were. But I froze."

"You're forgetting the outcome."

"What?"

"The killer would have shot the kid. No one but Pierce was injured. Remember that shooting in New York where nine bystanders were hit when the police fired on a shooter?"

"No."

"All of the bystanders were wounded by police bullets or bullet fragments. In your case only the shooter was hit. You're allowing the bullshit to mess with your mind. The family was saved. The killers are no longer a threat. That is all you really need to think about. All of the other stuff is bullshit." She picked up her burger and pointed at the soup. "Eat your lunch. You're not very sexy when your ribs start to show."

How much weight have I lost? He picked up the spoon and ate his soup.

×

Lori said, "Lane, it's me. You know I don't usually work on the weekends so you're gonna owe me for this one."

"Just a moment, please." Lane covered his left ear with his hand, held the phone closer to his ear, got up from the leather recliner to get away from the TV and went upstairs to the bedroom. He closed the door. "What's up?"

"Something. Jean's just not sure. Lots of calls coming into the chief's office from Edmonton. More than normal. She recognized one voice. It was Simpson's MLA."

"She is going to keep you informed?"

Lori chuckled. "You understand that none of this can be repeated to anyone?"

"Yes."

"She's got the feeling that something big is in the works.

She's just not sure exactly what it is. Nothing definite but her hunches have a tendency to be right. I hope that helps you."

"It does. Thank you."

"I like flowers. Big bouquets with lots of red, pink and yellow roses." Lori hung up.

×

Lane pushed the stroller. Indiana slept with his head leaning up against the side of the fabric. Sam's leash was tied to the handle on the left side. Lane felt himself getting into the rhythm of the walk as they passed in and out of the shade from the poplar trees lining the paved pathway.

His phone vibrated. He unbuttoned his shirt pocket, pulled out his phone, checked the number and pressed the green button. "Hello, Carlo."

"Detective Lane?"

"Yes. Have a good day with the truck?"

"Busy day. Just got it all scrubbed down and ready for tomorrow. Had an interesting conversation today."

Lane stopped under the shade and next to a parked pickup. He looked around to make sure no one was within earshot. Sam gave Lane a puzzled look, harrumphed, then sat. "Go ahead."

"A girl I used to go to school with dropped by for a calzone and told me that Mara used to hang out with a couple of guys named Rogerson and Bertoulli. Apparently another of their friends was killed in a fight. Someone hit the guy up the side of the head with a toilet seat. A month after that, the toilet seat killer was murdered in a drive-by. My friend told me there were three guys in the car. The story going around was that Mara was the shooter, Rogerson did the driving and Bertoulli handled the phone."

"How come she told you this?"

"She was a friend of Camille Desjardin at the time. I mentioned what happened to my grandmother and Camille, and she told me the drive-by story. It was like she wanted to help out."

Lane looked ahead as a woman driving a minivan sped through the playground zone. She talked, held a phone with her left hand and drove with her right.

"That helps. Thanks."

"Remember our bargain?"

"I remember."

"Good." Carlo hung up.

chapter 14

What's he doing here on his day off? Walter wondered. He watched Brett stroke Cora's hand.

The garden room was filled with family and inmates — at least, that's how Walter liked to refer to them. Lois, the crazy one in the wheelchair who was quite capable of walking, talked into a portable phone that everyone knew didn't work. She talked so loud that even Walter could hear her when she said, "She has a Mennonite boyfriend!" The young woman who came to visit Lois every Sunday looked at Walter, raised her eyebrows and smiled.

Penny sat next to him and tended to his nails. The manicure tingled the ends of his nerves, and he liked the warmth of her hand on his. He said, "I was thinking about Linda the other day."

Penny stopped buffing, turned to face him so he could see her lips, and asked, "Were you in Las Vegas?"

Walter nodded. "I'd just won big. She liked to gamble, you know."

Penny nodded and smiled. "She could always make you smile."

Walter lifted his chin in Cora's direction. "What's wrong with her?"

Penny looked over her shoulder, then turned back to face Walter before she said, "I don't know. Maybe Brett will be able to make her feel better."

"Where is Cora's eldest granddaughter?"

Penny set the emery board down. "I think she's gone for a holiday in Mexico."

Walter shuddered when he remembered the front-page picture of his daughter and the headline CALGARY WOMAN MURDERED IN MEXICO.

Penny's cheeks turned red and she watched Walter's face to read his expression. She touched his arm. "Sorry, Wally."

Walter shrugged and studied Cora's eyes while she watched Brett and nodded at what he was saying. Walter read her lips as she said, "I can get the money tomorrow."

Freddy McQuade rolled up beside Walter, who looked over at the ancient man and said, "I thought you were dead."

Freddy's weight had dropped to about one hundred twenty pounds. He reminded Walter of a Holocaust survivor wearing a Stephen Harper toupee. Freddy revealed a mouthful of whitened teeth, then said, "Fuck you, Wally! I'm havin' a good day!"

Walter smiled. Penny said, "Good to see you, Freddy."

"Not for long!"

Penny looked over at Brett, who was waving her closer. She got up and walked over to sit on the other side of Cora.

Walter reached inside his shirt and leaned close to Freddy. He held out the white fentanyl packet with the purple lettering. "I need another one!"

Freddy focused on the packet and watched as Walter tucked it away. He looked at his old friend and asked, "What for?"

Walter raised his eyebrows and smiled.

Freddy shrugged. "Okay."

×

Lane parked just in front of the yellow tape running from a fence post across the alley and around a telephone pole. The white-and-blue-striped forensics van was parked between two garages and another stretch of tape. They were one house south of the home Lane had grown up in. The detective got out of the Chev and looked over the fence at the corner window that had been his bedroom. He walked alongside the van. The soles of his shoes crunched on the gravel. Memories and their accompanying emotions were overwhelming.

"Over here."

Lane stopped and looked up at Fibre. He leaned on a cedar fence in his white bunny suit. "Find anything?" Lane asked.

"About one metre down. The mother told me the child was buried in a metal container. I used a metal detector. Didn't need ground radar like I first thought." Fibre pointed at a black body bag. It was flat at both ends but the middle was round.

My mother used to keep her flower and sugar in metal bins. "Was the container white?"

"Yes. It was white on the inside of the lid." Fibre studied Lane. "You look pale."

Lane inhaled slowly, then took as long to exhale. He looked up at the window of his room and had a flashback of his mother swinging the leather belt. His right hand felt for the small of his back. "I only asked her what happened to the baby."

"What?" Fibre asked.

Lane saw the hole in Pierce's eye socket after the bullet hit. He stepped back and put one hand on the hood of the van. There was a kind of brilliant haze in his eyes, making it impossible to see what was directly in front of him. It was followed by a powerful wave of nausea.

"Detective?"

Lane heard Fibre's voice. About thirty seconds later the doctor had Lane under the arms and was sitting him down. A sharp piece of gravel dug itself into Lane's right butt cheek. He lifted his cheek, dug out the stone and tossed it. It smacked against the fence.

It took twenty minutes for the medical examiner's van to arrive and for Fibre to return the scene to its former condition. He parked Lane's car out on the street, then drove the forensics unit van north and west. Lane sat in the passenger's seat with his hand over his eyes. He winced when the van hit a bump.

"The acetaminophen should help with the pain, but you still need to go home and sleep. When you wake up you will feel much better." Fibre turned onto Sarcee Trail and accelerated. "Do you get migraines very often?"

"Almost never." Lane peeked out between his fingers to see they were headed down the long hill into the Bow River valley. The pain was sharper now, and he closed his eyes. "I owe you."

"No, you don't."

Fifteen minutes later, Fibre pulled up in front of Lane's house, got out of the van and helped the detective up the stairs.

The door opened. Through the haze of pain, Lane heard Christine ask, "What do you want?"

"He's helping me out," Lane said.

Fibre said, "I think he has a migraine. I've given him acetaminophen. He needs rest."

Lane grabbed Christine's wrist. Her gentle and usually pleasing perfume almost made him gag. He covered his mouth. "Thank him for me, please."

"No way!"

She still remembers her fight with Fibre. Lane turned, opened his eyes, stepped out onto the front step and spotted Fibre at the front of the van. "Thank you!" Then Lane leaned over the railing and threw up into the juniper.

chapter 15

Police Chief Expected to Run in By-Election

Sources inside the Progressive Conservative party confirm Calgary's Police Chief Jim Simpson has been asked to run as their candidate in the upcoming by-election. The retirement of Bill Smith in Calgary Varsity had political watchers wondering who the PCs would select to replace him.

Simpson is considered a prime candidate because of his solid public reputation and ability to communicate with media.

Unconfirmed reports suggest the Premier is looking to replace solicitor general Bill Rogerson, who has embarrassed the government with a private member's bill that has drawn strong opposition. Party insiders say Simpson's law and order credentials make him an excellent contender as a replacement, should he win the by-election.

×

"You look like shit!" Terri ran her own coffee kiosk on the Stephen Avenue Mall. She offered unsolicited comments that often shocked and sometimes entertained. She frowned at Lane from behind her espresso machine.

"I'm actually feeling a bit better." Lane looked over his shoulder to see the next person in line — a hefty guy in a black suit — was smiling. Lane blinked slowly. His sunglasses were taking the edge off the intense morning sun.

"The usual?" Terri.

"Please." Lane handed over a bill. Terri took it, then went to work her magic with a flash of polished steel, the rumble of a grinder and a hiss of steam.

Terri handed over Lane's moccaccino and said, "You should go home."

"This will help." Lane smiled, lifted his cup and headed down the mall. When he walked into the office, Lori looked up, leaned back in her chair and looked at him sideways. He lifted his eyebrows, said, "Mornin'," then headed into his office where he set his cup down, hung up his jacket and sat down gingerly.

Lori stood in the doorway with her hands on her hips, wearing a new white dress and a pair of black pumps. She waited.

"I think I had a migraine yesterday."

"You think?"

"I couldn't see and my eyes still hurt."

Lori nodded. "You had a migraine. You look like —"

"— shit. Terri told me that already."

"The coffee lady?"

Don't nod. Your brain feels like it's bruised. "That's right."

"If the shoe fits." Lori looked over her shoulder. "Did you read this morning's paper?"

"No."

"It looks like Simpson is moving into provincial politics."

Lori frowned. "Just when this place was getting back into some kind of shape."

Lane reached for his coffee as Nigel walked in. He asked, "Going old school with those Wayfarers?"

×

Walter tried for the thirty-second time to tear open the fentanyl packet. He stared at his purple swollen hands and wished he had the use of them again for maybe thirty seconds. All it would take would be a thumb and a forefinger. He looked at the TV where the top ten catches of this baseball season were being replayed.

Two toes and the front end of a wheelchair entered the room. The driver misjudged and scraped the wall. The bottom half of Freddy's face appeared. The Stephen Harper toupee flopped over and covered his eyes. He used his right hand to push the toupee back into place, then backed up and made a successful run into the room. Freddy looked at Walter. "Got another one for you!"

Walter nodded and tried to smile as he used his fists to push himself up in bed.

Freddy manoeuvred the chair alongside Walter's bed and crashed into the frame. The bed shifted one way and Walter nearly tumbled out the other side.

Freddy said, "Here! Let me help you with that!" He took the fentanyl packet from Walter, ripped the top off, then handed the packet to Walter. "The last couple of days I've been feelin' pretty chipper. The pain is givin' me a break and I don't need the hallucinations these things give me!" He threw another open packet on Walter's lap.

Walter looked at the fentanyl patch. "How do these damned things work?"

"Let me know exactly what you're up to and I'll show you."

Nigel looked over his partner's shoulder at the map Lane had put together on his big screen. He pointed at the image of a food truck. Nigel said, "We haven't heard from Carlo. Should I give him a call and see if he's found out anything more about the connection between Rogerson, Brett and MCSC?"

Lane nodded. "Good idea."

Nigel reached for his phone sitting at the corner of his desk. "I'll do that right now."

Lane used the mouse to work his way around the map, then shrank the image so it fit inside the screen. There were still at least thirty seniors residences they had yet to visit with no guarantee Brett Mara would be found at any of them. He leaned back in his chair and eased his head gingerly from side to side to release a bit of tension. There was still a bit of tenderness behind his eyeballs. His appetite hadn't returned, but he felt better.

Nigel pressed end on his phone. "I'll try texting Carlo." His fingers did a dance on the phone's face.

"You up for a drive?" Lane leaned forward, put his palms on the desk and stood up slowly.

✕

Brett poked his head inside Walter's room. He wore a navy-blue top and pants. Walter took a long breath to steady his nerves. Brett held up a couple of fresh white towels, looked at his watch, set the towels at the foot of the bed, put one finger in front of his face and left.

Walter waited for thirty seconds then checked the fentanyl patches Freddy had taped to the insides of his forearms. They were close to the crooks of his elbows, where he felt he still retained some power in his arms.

×

Lane's phone rang as they travelled west along 4th Avenue, then over the Louise Bridge. He picked the phone out of his jacket pocket, glanced at the number, looked sideways at Nigel, pressed the green button and held the phone a few centimetres from his ear. "Lane here."

Harper said, "The rumours are true."

Lane asked, "We're being played?"

"If we are, then the game is much bigger than I expected and the stakes just got higher. Thought you might want a heads-up. Looks like the premier or her party caught wind of Rogerson's old gang connection before we did."

"It does look that way."

Harper asked, "You all right? You sound a little off."

"I'm okay."

"Any news on your end?"

"Not yet."

"Keep in touch. Oh, and it looks like Simpson is making a move." Harper hung up.

×

Walter took long slow breaths. *I hope I can hang on.*

A figure in a dark-grey business suit walked into the room. His hair was styled and gelled into deliberate disarray. His eyebrows were dyed the same shade of black as his hair. His beard was trimmed and sculpted to accentuate a weak jaw line. There was an electric blue tie at his throat. He smiled.

Walter's eyes glanced to the right where his daughter's picture leaned on the end table. He closed his eyes and remembered the headline: MURDERED IN MEXICO. He opened his eyes and saw Robbie pick up Linda's photo. He remembered what she'd said the day before she'd left for

Cancun. "Dad, I'm thinking that when I get back I'll be looking for my own place. Do you think I could borrow the money for a down payment?"

Walter looked at Robbie and watched his former son-in-law's lips moving. "Just thought I'd drop by and say hello." There was a new white gold wedding band on his finger. "Wally, we never were very close but we were family."

Family doesn't do what you did! Walter thought. He glanced at the fentanyl patch on his left arm and rolled his forearm so it wouldn't be visible to Robbie. Then he resumed watching Robbie's lips.

Robbie said, "Since Linda died, I've gotten on with my life." He reached for the inside pocket of his suit jacket. "These are some papers I need you to sign, Wally." Robbie's fingers opened the folds.

Walter saw the words "Enduring Power of Attorney." He smiled. *I had my will rewritten four months ago. All that I have left goes to the Children's Hospital. But you don't know that!*

Robbie smiled and pulled a silver pen from his shirt pocket. "It's time for you and me to make amends."

Walter waved Robbie over. *Come closer.*

Robbie frowned and looked down at the paper-thin man, then forced a smile. He put the document on the bed, placed his right fist onto the edge of the mattress and leaned forward.

Walter hooked one elbow around Robbie's neck and then added the other arm to complete the lock. He worked his arms so that the patches rubbed against the skin under either of Robbie's ears. The old man caught the heavy scent of Robbie's cologne.

Robbie jerked back, pulling Walter out of bed. The old man tightened his grip and closed his eyes. Robbie fell back against the wall. Walter felt the shock of the blow against his right elbow. *Hang on!*

Walter held his breath and felt his heart pounding.

Then he felt a corner of the bed tear at the skin covering his shoulder blade. It cut him down to the bone. He hung on as Robbie rolled and the pair of them fell onto the floor. Wally closed his eyes, imagining Linda's smile.

×

"This the place?" Nigel parked in front of a two-storey red brick home on Briar Hill. Lane saw that although the neighbourhood was more than seventy years old, this house might have been built two years ago. Its white-framed windows and stained-glass door spoke of custom design. The twenty-metre epoxy pebble driveway was done in a deep shade of red to complement the brick. Lane opened his door. "She lives here?" Nigel asked.

Lane walked up the driveway, then the front steps. The door opened before he could ring the bell.

Gloria was dressed in jeans and a white T-shirt.

"I have news." Lane looked inside and saw Gloria's niece walking along the hallway to stand behind her aunt.

"You found her?" Gloria looked over Lane's shoulder as Nigel climbed the stairs.

"Yes. The body is at the medical examiner's. I've asked that it be released to you after examination."

Gloria patted her right hand on her sternum. Her eyes filled with tears. "Can you come in?"

Lane's phone rang. He pulled it out of his pocket, looked at the number and gave Gloria an apologetic look. "I have to take this." He pressed a button.

Lori said, "They need you at Bow Valley. It's just over the bridge in Bowness. It's a seniors residence. Dr. Weaver is already on his way."

"Thanks." Lane hung up and looked at Gloria. "I have to go." He frowned and tried to think through the after-fog of the migraine. "You have my number?"

Gloria tried to smile and nodded. Her niece put an arm around her aunt's shoulders.

"I..." Lane began. "I'll have to get back to you."

He felt a hand grip his bicep. Nigel said, "We have an emergency." He led Lane back down the stairs, leaned him up against the side of the Chev, opened the door and backed his partner into the seat. He ran around the front of the car, got in and started the engine. They did up their seat belts as he drove downhill to Parkdale Boulevard.

Nigel crossed over the Bow River, slowed and turned left at a brown brick two-storey building fronted by mature evergreens.

A black-and-white police car was parked out front and an officer stood at the door. "All entrances and exits are covered," she said.

"Thanks," Lane said as they opened the double doors and entered the main building. In front of them was a hallway leading to a garden with a two-storey roof and skylights. A hutch with rabbits stood to the left, and cheerful red-and-white decorations evoked a Canada Day theme. A woman in a wheelchair rolled past them, stopped, picked up the phone on the coffee table and said, "She's got a Mennonite boyfriend!"

"I didn't see her dial," Nigel said.

"She didn't." Lane squinted through his post-migraine haze and saw a brown-haired woman in a black knee-length skirt and jacket turn the corner. Her heels made an important announcement as they approached. "Here comes the manager."

"Mr. Lane?" she asked, and when he nodded, she indicated he should follow. "I'm Colleen."

As they turned the corner in the hallway an approaching nurse in a blue shirt and pants turned to tap the screen of a flat-screen computer.

Lane felt Nigel's thumb in his ribs. *What the hell is your problem?* Lane thought.

Colleen passed the man in blue, then turned right and stopped at a closed door. "Once we determined that both were deceased, I ordered the room closed and left undisturbed. An inspector was here and confirmed that this is a homicide."

Lane nodded at Colleen, who had short brown hair, brown eyes and a beaked nose. *She looks like she's about to cry,* Lane thought.

"Walter was a friend," she said as she read his reaction.

"I think it's him." Nigel tapped Lane on the shoulder.

Who? Lane heard the sound of clogs on the concrete floor. "What?"

Nigel said, "Hold on!" then ran back down the hall the way they'd come.

Lane turned. "What the hell's going on, Nigel?" He pointed to his right. "The bodies are over here."

The man in blue was running. He wore clogs with spring-loaded heels. As the nurse approached the corner, one clog came off and the other heel skidded. The man fell onto his right hip, then crashed feet first into the wall. A couple of sheets of coloured paper fluttered to the floor.

Lane trotted up the hall and stood over Nigel. Nigel had the man in blue face down on the floor, his knee planted in the man's back. Lane grabbed one wrist and locked it with a handcuff; then he grabbed the other arm and finished the job. Lane swallowed hard when the floor began to shimmy. He breathed deeply to quell the nausea.

Nigel rolled the man over, sat him up and pushed his back to the wall. Looking up at Lane, he said, "This is Brett Mara."

The man in blue shook his head. "No, I'm not."

Lane closed his eyes, opened them again and looked at the face of the man he'd last seen on a tour bus in Cuba.

Colleen stood at Lane's elbow and looked from Brett to the detectives. She opened her mouth and then closed it.

Another woman arrived. She had tightly curled white hair and wore stretchy brown pants and a floral patterned sweatshirt. If she weighed one hundred pounds, it would only be after a Thanksgiving dinner. She held a cheque in the air and waved it. "What are you doing to him? He saved my life. He's the one who can save my granddaughter and my great-grandkids! They're in Mexico! I have to give him this cheque or they won't be able to get out of jail!"

Colleen's eyes narrowed, then focused on Brett. She turned to the white-haired woman. "Come with me, Cora. Your granddaughter left me with an emergency contact number. Let's see if we can talk with her before you hand over that cheque."

Twenty minutes later, Lane looked at the photograph of Walter on the wall next to the door handle leading to his room. The detective knocked.

"Just one moment!" Fibre said.

Lane looked down the hall where a round woman in a fuchsia top and pants pushed a man in a wheelchair. She looked up at Lane. He saw her hair was tied in a ponytail at the back. She studied the detective as he watched her. She turned the wheelchair, rolled the man into his room and disappeared.

Fibre opened the door and nodded at Lane. "What?"

"If you have time, I need preliminary observations."

Fibre rubbed the top of his white bunny suit's hood. "Why?"

"I have a suspect to interview."

"Oh." Fibre looked over his shoulder. "It appears that the resident taped fentanyl patches to the insides of his wrists."

"Fentanyl?"

"About a hundred times stronger than morphine. It's frequently indicated for cancer patients in palliative care."

"Did Walter have cancer?" Lane looked past Fibre, taking in the room. Both beds were pushed against the far wall. An elderly man lay face up on the floor, his eyes open, a white film of froth around his lips. A younger man in a grey business suit was curled up with his back to the older man. The ripped curtain dividing the room in half hung from two hooks. Pillows, pictures and bits of plastic and glass from a flat-screen TV completed the chaotic scene.

Fibre shook his head. "Don't know. He appears to have died from myocardial infarction, while the younger man may have died from an overdose of fentanyl. It will take a tox report to confirm that. There is evidence of a prolonged and violent struggle between the men. Those are my preliminary findings."

Lane lifted his chin. "Thanks." Fibre shut the door. The detective took his time turning to the right. His eyes were slow to focus and any movement threatened to induce another bout of nausea.

"Are you the police?"

Lane stopped and turned around. The woman with the long ponytail stood in front of him. She was a head shorter than the detective. "Yes."

"That's Wally's ex-son-in-law in there. Robbie. I saw him go in to see Wally earlier. Wally told me his daughter Linda was going to leave Robbie after they got back from Mexico, but she died down there. Wally blamed Robbie for her death. Said he murdered her down there and got away with it."

Lane tried to place the woman's accent. "Who are you?"

"Penny. I looked after Wally. He talked to me. His wife died four or five years ago. Then his daughter. Wally was very lonely."

"Do you know the son-in-law's last name?"

"Van Leenan."

Lane took out his pen and wrote the name on his left palm. "Do you have a cell phone?"

Penny reached into the pocket of her uniform top and handed it to Lane, who said, "I just need the number, please."

She told it to him and he wrote it down on his palm under Robbie's last name. "I will need to interview you later."

Penny shrugged as she put her phone back into her pocket. "I'm a Canadian citizen now, so I'm not worried." She looked over her shoulder. "Mrs. Wong needs me."

Lane nodded. "I'll get back to you." He eased himself around her and went down the hall to find Nigel.

×

Lane sat in one corner of the interrogation room. Brett Mara sat in another. He still wore his spring-loaded clogs and his blue shirt and pants. He studied Lane with his green eyes.

Lane looked at the red file he had face down on the tiny table in front of him. He turned to look over his left shoulder and up at the camera. "Just to confirm, you have agreed to talk without a lawyer present?"

Brett nodded and stretched his six-foot frame. "These chairs are uncomfortable."

"Kind of get me right here after a while." Lane eased his right arm around to touch his lower back.

Brett smiled. His brown hair was tipped with blond highlights.

He's confident and he doesn't recognize me from Cuba. "Just want to clear up a few things. Cora from the seniors residence says that you saved her life?"

Brett leaned forward. "That's right. After she regained consciousness, she asked, 'Am I in hell?' It was hilarious." He laughed.

You like having power over life and death. "Also, you were scheduled to bathe Walter Riley this morning."

"That's correct."

"You've worked at Bow Valley for how long?"

"About two weeks."

"And before that?"

Brett looked at the ceiling as if trying to remember. "I had my own window-washing company."

Lane nodded. *Just pretend you believe him.* "Did you enjoy your vacation in Havana?"

Brett looked at Lane and smiled. "This is where this whole misunderstanding confuses me. I'd sure like to go to Cuba, but I haven't had the pleasure."

Lane turned over a photograph and handed it to Brett. "Just to refresh your memory. This is a picture of you and Camille on a street in Havana."

Brett looked at the photograph. "Sure looks like me, but it isn't me. My father got around, you know. People keep telling me I look like someone else. Guess dad made a trip to Cuba and I have a half-brother there."

Lane stood up and taped the photograph to the wall. He turned over another and handed it Brett. "This is you shoving Camille into a moto volqueta."

Brett feigned disinterest as he took the photo, then held it closer. He tossed the photo onto the table. "Like I said, that's not me."

"She died of her injuries."

"Very unfortunate."

Lane turned over another photograph. "This was taken by Cuban Immigration after your flight landed at Varadero airport."

Brett crossed his arms and yawned.

"I can testify I was on the bus with you on the tour of Havana."

Brett looked directly at Lane. "You must be mistaken."

Lane stood up and taped the photographs to the wall.

"I also have statements from families of elderly residents of various seniors facilities who say you killed their parents or grandparents." He lifted the documents and taped them to the wall.

Brett shrugged his shoulders. "Like I keep saying, it wasn't me."

Lane took a Sharpie pen, then a blank piece of paper, and wrote MONSTER across it. He stuck it to the wall.

"I'm not a monster," Brett said.

"I've talked with some of the families and they think you are."

"They weren't there like I was. Some of them only visited once a month if that."

Gotcha! Lane passed Brett another document. "You are an investor with Mi Casa Su Casa."

"Those guys are the monsters, not me. They prey on the elderly. Half of my patients asked me to help them die. They were depressed and when they were lucid, they wanted me to help them die."

You just can't help yourself, can you, Brett? You have to get in the last word, and you don't like being called a monster. "Circle the names of the ones who asked you to help them die." Lane handed Brett a list of names and a pencil. The killer began circling.

×

Nigel and Lane walked along the Stephen Avenue Mall. The older detective wore sunglasses and walked on the shady side.

Nigel asked, "You happy with the way the interrogation is going?"

Lane nodded. "The next step is to get him to turn on Rogerson." He turned to Nigel. "You've got the sworn statements and the banking information?"

Nigel nodded. "All done up in bar graphs so they'll be easy to read."

"Thanks, and thanks again for spotting Mara. I walked right past him." Lane spotted Terri's coffee kiosk set on the shady side of the avenue. "This migraine has me in a bit of a fog."

Nigel pointed further down the mall. "Want to try a food truck? Looks like Steakout is here."

"Not really hungry. You go ahead. I'll get the coffees."

Nigel stepped out into the sun and walked down the mall. Lane got in line for a cup of coffee. He watched short-haired Terri as she took orders, handed out coffees, worked her magic with the espresso machine and banged the used coffee grounds against a metal bar. The tail end of the lunch-hour crowd was checking the time. A few butted out cigarettes.

"You've got some colour back. Why didn't you go home?" Terri asked as he handed her a twenty and she handed back the change. He dropped a loonie in the tip cup.

He shrugged. "Something's come up."

"You're a detective, right?"

Lane studied Terri, who was measuring and tamping coffee grounds for a moccaccino and a latte, then looked over his shoulder. "That's right."

"It was good what you did to save that family in January. Anyone can see what it's cost you, but what other choice was there?" Terri locked the portafilter and set two small cups under it. She turned on the steam. It screamed then gurgled as she heated the milk. "You gotta ask yourself what woulda happened if you hadn't been there because that professor and his hairdresser wife killed so many others."

"I still don't feel right about what I had to do." *Why did you say that?*

Terri poured the espresso into a pair of paper cups, added the steamed milk, then squirted chocolate into one, stirred it with a long-handled spoon and passed both over. She held onto the cups as Lane took hold of them and said, "Of course killing someone doesn't *feel* right. That's because you have a conscience." She released the cups. "You wouldn't expect to feel any other way, but you have to admit that you did what needed to be done."

The next customer placed an order. Lane went to sit on a shaded bench. He watched people as they got up and headed back to work. Nigel joined him a few minutes later with his prime rib on a bun. Lane sipped his moccaccino and handed the latte to Nigel. Nigel polished off the prime rib, then wiped his fingertips with a napkin. "What's next?"

"Remind me to call Deylis and let her know what's happened."

✕

Lori leaned left and eyed Lane from behind her computer screen. "Is there a reason why you left your phone in the office?"

Lane tapped his jacket pocket, rolled his eyes and winced. "Shit."

"Ben Bertoulli wants an appointment ASAP." Lori stood up. "His words, not mine. He'll be here in thirty minutes."

The big-time defence lawyer with the eyes that seem to look in two directions at once. The bulbous nose that arrests attention. And the whitened teeth meant for accentuating distractions. "You're joking."

"Nope. The guy who drives cops, prosecutors, judges and juries crazy is on his way to see you. Can't wait to meet him in the flesh." Lori shook her head. "Someone hired the big gun to defend Mara."

Nigel trailed Lane into the office. "What's up?"

"You have thirty minutes to find out all you can about Ben Bertoulli. I especially want to know if he has any elderly relatives in seniors facilities. While you're doing that, I've got some calls to make." Lane opened the door to their office, set down his coffee, took off his jacket and hung it on the back of the door. Then he picked up his phone and dialed. "Could I speak with Tommy, please?"

×

Ben Bertoulli smiled and shook hands with Nigel, Lane and Harper when they met in the conference room. He took off his blue pinstriped suit jacket and hung it on the back of the chair. He left it with the label showing above the chair back. Lane read the label: *Ozwald Boateng No. 30 Savile Row*. Bertoulli turned one eye to spot Lane inspecting the suit and flashed his whitened teeth. The expression seemed out of place. "You should go to London, Mr. Lane. You look like a man who would appreciate a fine suit."

Lane smiled. "You should go to Havana, Mr. Bertoulli. You look like a man who might enjoy a mojito." He sat down on one side of the table. *Tommy said the best way to handle Bertoulli is to keep him off balance and say things that are a bit vague, that suggest you know more than you're telling.* Harper sat at one end, Bertoulli at the other, Nigel across from Lane. Nigel opened his laptop.

Bertoulli took a moment to roll up the sleeves of his white shirt so everyone could see the BB monogram on the tailored cuffs.

Harper noticed the monogrammed shirt, then looked at Lane as if to say, *You've got to be kidding!*

Lane said, "You called this meeting, Mr. Bertoulli."

Ben leaned forward and hid his hands under the table.

Tommy said Bertoulli's hands are a giveaway. If he tucks them under the table, he wants to deal. If he locks them and puts them on the table in front of him, he thinks he has you by the balls.

Bertoulli said, "I think we can avoid a trial and save the taxpayers the expense. My client is willing to plead guilty to one charge of fraud."

Lane nodded at Nigel, who pointed at the Smart board on the wall. "We have sworn statements from two families whose loved ones removed large sums of money from their accounts. The same sums then appeared as deposits in three accounts under three aliases belonging to your client." Nigel tapped the enter key. A series of cancelled cheques appeared in sequence on the screen. "We also discovered that the occurrence of myocardial infarction spiked while your client worked at a series of institutions. These events followed withdrawals of between twenty and thirty thousand dollars from accounts belonging to the deceased residents."

Lane turned to Bertoulli. "We understand that your grandmother is a resident in a seniors residence in Edgemont?"

"I fail to see the relevance." Bertoulli raised his eyebrows while he appeared to be looking at Lane and Nigel at the same time.

Nigel continued. "We also have a series of photographs that show Mr. Mara pushing a woman into a piece of construction equipment in Havana." The image flashed on the screen. Brett Mara's profile was clear, as was his extended arm and Camille Mara tumbling into the bucket of the moto volqueta. "This document verifies that Mr. Mara is wanted in Havana for murder."

Harper said, "Our evidence suggests that you are defending a murderer who defrauded elderly patients and then killed them. He also killed Camille Mara because she knew about his operations and threatened to expose him. We will be charging your client with multiple counts of murder and fraud." Harper stood up. "The Crown Prosecutor will arrive momentarily to advise you on the details of the charges."

Ben held up his hands with the palms facing Harper. "Is that really necessary? Your evidence is obviously circumstantial."

Lane nodded at Nigel, who pressed a button on his computer to replay Brett Mara's recorded confession. Lane's voice said, "You are an investor with Mi Casa Su Casa."

Brett's recorded voice said, "Those guys are the monsters, not me. Half of my patients asked me to help them die. They were depressed and when they were lucid, they wanted me to help them die."

Harper opened the door. "Your client gave us a list of names of people he 'helped to die.' Fraud is the least of his worries, and yours since you invested with Mr. Mara. Your partner is a serial killer."

Lane stood up and nodded at Ben's suit jacket. "Don't forget to take your jacket with you." He and Nigel followed Harper out the door.

✕

The four met in Harper's office. They stared at the cell phone set on the middle of the knee-high coffee table.

Lori said, "Gee, this is about as exciting as watching John in front of the TV when the Super Bowl is on. No, I'm not running to the store for chips and beer."

Nigel chuckled, looked out the window and asked, "You really think Bertoulli is part of the MCSC deal?"

Harper undid the top button of his shirt. "We'll know soon."

Lane took a long slow breath. "He paid at least five thousand for that suit. My jacket cost less than two hundred on sale. A trip to London for the fitting, staying in a fine hotel, meals, airfare, taxis. That's serious money. Besides, he went to school with Mara and Rogerson. He was also in the car with them when they did their drive-by." He nodded at Lori.

Harper got up and stepped behind his desk. "So you think Bertoulli'll give up Mara to protect his own ass? We may be here for a while. How about some pizza?"

"These guys work by a different set of rules." Lane stood up and looked out of the window. Below, the street was choked with vehicles. "They look after number one first. And it's about status and the lifestyle. Rogerson and Bertoulli will see Mara as a threat now. They'll be in damage-control mode. We know about Mara's operation. They'll cut him loose before we can connect all three of them to the MCSC deal. Being connected to a serial killer is bad for business. Their MCSC partners will want no part of this because they are already facing a class-action lawsuit in the States. There will be phone calls back and forth, but a cutting of ties with Brett Mara is inevitable."

chapter 16

Legislative Insiders Say Calgary Police Chief Will Accept Nomination

Calgary Police Service Chief Jim Simpson has accepted the nomination to run as the Progressive Conservative candidate in next month's by-election in Calgary Varsity.

Simpson himself has not made a public statement, but his office says a formal announcement of his plans can be expected shortly.

If elected, Simpson has been widely touted as the replacement for solicitor general Bill Rogerson, thought to be out of favour with the premier. Recent controversy over a private member's bill introduced by Rogerson has caused the government considerable embarrassment.

Opponents insist the bill allows private companies to exploit the province's elderly. One of these companies, Mi Casa Su Casa, is facing a class-action lawsuit in the United States involving the surviving families of more than 300 former MCSC residents. The plaintiffs seek $1.5 billion US in damages.

×

Lane woke up to Norah Jones. He rolled over and shut off the clock radio so Arthur could sleep in. He expected to feel pain behind his eyes and was relieved that it was gone.

After a coffee, quick breakfast and shower, he headed out the door and walked to the LRT station. As he walked by the schoolyard, a coyote crossed the street in front of him. The grey-and-tan neighbour paid Lane absolutely no attention. At the station Lane waited, enjoying his anonymity, and watched people in their crowded cocoons of thought.

The sun shone on his face so he wore his sunglasses on the ride downtown. He checked the time and headed for Terri's kiosk. The morning air was refreshing. He could see her face from a block away and she was ready with his moccaccino when he handed her a five. She handed him the change. "You look a lot better today."

Lane smiled, sipped and lifted his cup. "Thank you."

He found himself alone when he entered the office, sat down and logged onto his computer. He pulled up the map of the Mara case and scanned the various bits of the investigation.

There was a knock at the door. Lane looked up and saw the close-cropped hair, the narrow face and the smile of Chief Simpson, who wore a blue sport shirt and pants. "Just dropped by to say hello."

Lane stood up, then sat down when Simpson closed the door and sat in Nigel's chair. Lane asked, "What's up?"

"I already told Cam. Now I'm telling you. I've resigned." Simpson started to tap his left hand on Nigel's desk.

Lane waited. *He's got something more to say. Keep quiet and let him say it.*

Simpson moved his lips side to side as if chewing on the words. "When Smoke resigned, the guys in the Scotch drinkers' club thought he'd done it to himself."

Where's this going?

"Rogerson is another matter. His position gave the good ol' boys plenty of clout because of their connection to him. Your investigation has made the boys in the club nervous. They're afraid of what you might dig up about them." Simpson looked at Lane for a moment. "I thought I'd better let you know because the ol' boys like being in power. Now that the premier is a woman and not playing by their rules, there is likely to be fallout. You might become one of their targets. Keep your eyes open. If I get elected, I should have more clout to make situations like this a little less likely."

"Have you heard about anything coming this way?" Lane asked.

"Nothing specific. These things tend to blindside you. Some of these guys play the game the way Smoke did."

"I've been thinking in a different direction."

"Go ahead."

"The MCSC deal would make a great deal of money for those involved. Having the deal connected to a mass murderer will ruin reputations. The information I'm working on says Mara holds some incriminating evidence that will tarnish anyone connected to the deal. The loss of investment and the potential loss of status for those names revealed as MCSC investors —"

"— puts Mara's life at risk. Seems kind of —"

Lane nodded. "— ironic."

Simpson smiled. "It is that. Mara had such a callous disregard for life. Now he is expendable." He got up and shook Lane's hand. "There will be a formal announcement. I wanted to give you a heads-up first."

✕

Nigel and Anna sat across from each other in his kitchen. The house was nestled between 14th and 10th Streets, just across the river from downtown. The kitchen had white granite countertops and walnut cabinets separated with bright multicoloured Mexican tiles.

Anna wore a grey T-shirt and pajama bottoms. Nigel wore a light-blue shirt and navy-blue pants. Anna pulled her hair together and tucked it back. "I took a close look at MCSC."

"Lane said he didn't want you anywhere near that." Nigel shook his head.

"I know. You know what I do. I'm good at getting in and out of sites undetected. When you were talking about the connections between those three guys, I got curious and started to check a few things." Anna went over to the coffee pot to top up her cup. "You know that I've gone after some pretty unethical bastards. Well, these particular bastards are right up there." She lifted her free hand above her head for effect.

"How so?"

"The seniors buy their apartments starting at just under two hundred thousand dollars. After that, they pay for any service provided. When the senior dies, the money they used to purchase the apartment goes back to MCSC." Anna pulled out an oak chair, lifted her knees, sat yoga style and sipped her coffee. "Then they sell the apartment to the next person and begin again." Anna pointed a finger at Nigel. "After they are charged for repainting, cleaning and moving expenses."

"So it's a cash machine for investors." Nigel looked out the window.

"And a money-laundering machine. Brett Mara was close to becoming a major shareholder in this publicly traded company. So was Bertoulli. I couldn't find any evidence linking Rogerson to MCSC, though."

"It's looking like his connection is either a kickback as a reward for the private member's bill or he's being black-mailed into fronting for MCSC."

"Whatever the connection is, Bertoulli and Rogerson and all of the other investors have a whole lot to lose if someone shines a spotlight on MCSC." She hesitated and set down her coffee. "I've gone ahead and done something."

Nigel lifted his eyebrows.

"Remember my contacts at YYC News?"

Nigel exhaled. "No."

Anna lifted her eyebrows.

"You didn't."

"I did. YYC will look into this and we both know what they'll find." Anna lifted her cup and drained the remains of the coffee.

Nigel took a long, deep breath and let it out slowly. "I hope you're right."

×

Lori stood in Lane's doorway. She pushed her fingers back through her blonde hair. "What? Sometimes a girl needs a little time in the morning to brush her hair! There's someone to see you."

Lane frowned, threw his empty coffee cup at the garbage and missed. Then he got up, tugged at his missing earlobe, picked up the cup, threw it in the can and followed Lori.

Gloria with the violet eyes stood with her hands on a voluminous purse. She nodded and smiled tentatively.

Lane said, "Come on in," and took her by the elbow. She smelled of berries and soap. He pulled out Nigel's chair so she could sit, shut the door and sat down. "What's up?"

"I went to the funeral home and made arrangements. They contacted the medical examiner, who expects to release the body on Wednesday. The funeral home director said that the ME told them you had made a request that sped up the process. I came here to thank you and to invite you to the memorial on Friday." Gloria took a tissue out of her pants pocket and wiped at her eyes.

Lane waited.

She looked at him, and he saw a tear had made a translucent spot on her white blouse. "I thought the grief would go away, but it never has. But this—" She waved the tissue at him and waited for the words to come. "I'm sleeping better for the first time. I haven't slept through the night for so long —" she rubbed her eyebrows with her thumb and forefinger "— that I was a bit shocked when I woke up this morning and the sun was shining through a gap in the curtains. I'd slept right through the night. I wanted you to know what a difference you've made."

"I wish I could have somehow helped you when the baby was crying." Lane looked at his left knee as it danced. He tried to hold it still with his left hand.

"My mother was the one who needed to be held accountable. Not you." She pointed at him, then herself. "Not me."

"What happened to her?"

"She died in her sleep about a year ago."

Lane nodded.

Gloria looked at Lane's bouncing knee. "I know my brothers and I weren't the only ones scarred by what happened to my daughter."

Lane stared back at her and felt tightness in his chest. He could not speak because he could not breathe.

Gloria handed him another tissue. "I didn't come here to upset you. I came here to thank you."

Lane took the tissue, wiped his eyes and took a long, shuddering breath. "You're right. It never goes away."

"But it does get better."

About ten minutes after Gloria left, Lori stepped into Lane's office. "You okay?"

He nodded.

"Can I ask what that was about?"

Lane motioned for her to sit, took a breath and told her the story.

When he'd finished, she asked, "And you're going to the memorial?"

"I think so, as long as work doesn't get in the way."

"Speaking of work, what are we going to do now that Simpson is going? The good old boys think this is an opening for them."

He leaned his head to the right. *Lori always knows what's going on.* "Maybe and maybe not. This other case we're working on may have them running for the shadows."

"Tell me more. Maybe I can help."

✕

Nigel walked into the interrogation room with coffees and a smile. "Moccaccino for you." He set one cup in front of Lane. "And vanilla latte for you." He set the second cup in front of Brett Mara, who wore an orange jumpsuit. Mara nodded and picked up the coffee. Nigel backed out the door.

Lane loosened his red tie, hung his grey jacket on the back of his chair, then sat down and sipped his coffee. "You wanted to talk?"

Brett nodded and put his cup down. "Thanks for the coffee." He looked up at Lane. "I want to tell my story."

"Okay." *Why the change?*

"Ben dropped me as a client."

Lane nodded.

"They put a Kevlar vest on me when they brought me here." Brett looked at the camera. He swiped at a spot on his orange leg.

Lane waited.

"Me, Bertoulli and Rogerson were friends in high school."

Lane nodded.

"Before I talk about them, what can you do for me?"

"If you're asking for a deal, you need a lawyer."

"I want a deal with you. I want you to make a promise."

Lane tipped his chin down and watched Brett out of his left eye.

"I want you to promise that Sonja will be able to go home."

"Who is Sonja?" Lane asked.

"My Cuban wife."

Lane frowned. "Did she enter the country legally?"

He shook his head. "No."

"She could be deported."

"Nope. That's not acceptable. She needs a plane ticket home."

"I will see what can be done."

Brett smiled. "And I want my story out there."

Lane shrugged his shoulders. "I can't make any promises about that."

Brett leaned forward. "But you will see what can be done?"

Lane nodded. "I will."

"Okay, then. Ask your questions."

"If I think you're lying to me, I'm out the door and all deals will be off."

Brett nodded.

"What happened in Havana the day you were on the tour with Camille?"

"The day I pushed her into the moto volqueta?"

"Yes."

"She pissed me off. She was fucking my friend and rubbing my nose in it on the bus. When I said something to her, she asked, 'What are you going to do about it?' When I saw the chance I went ahead and shoved her. It was spur-of-the-moment stuff. The opportunity presented itself so I took it." Brett reached for his coffee, sat back and sipped.

We could be discussing the weather. He is very matter of fact.

"Then you killed her boyfriend?"

Brett nodded. "That's right."

"How did you get out of Cuba?"

Brett smiled. "If you have the money, you can get a ride on a boat."

"Out of Matanzas?"

"That's one way out. There are others."

"Sonja travelled with you from Matanzas to the US?"

"That's right."

So you killed Camille for screwing around and don't see the hypocrisy of your prior relationship with Sonja. "Is she in Calgary now?"

Brett nodded.

"Where exactly?"

"In my motorhome. It's parked in a Walmart parking lot. You wouldn't believe what campgrounds charge per day."

So that's what made you so hard to find. You were hiding in plain sight. "Which one?"

"Signal Hill."

Nigel will be on that. Lane didn't turn to look at the camera. Instead he looked at Brett. "What can you tell me about Mrs. Leandro?"

"She was one of my patients." Brett revealed neither anxiety nor boredom on his face or in his tone of voice.

"How did she die?"

"I smothered her."

"How come?"

"I told her that her grandson was travelling and in trouble. She gave me fifty-five thousand dollars to get him out of trouble. Then he walked in the door one day. I had to shut her up and move on."

"How about Mrs. Po at Floral Gardens?"

"Same kind of scam. She paid me fifty thousand. I gave her an overdose of insulin."

"How many in total did you kill?"

Brett concentrated and began counting on his fingers. "Including the guy I killed in high school?"

Lane nodded.

"Twenty-seven."

Fatigue settled itself on Lane's shoulders and it took a deep breath to keep them from sagging. He handed Brett a sheet of paper and a pen. "I'd like you to write a second list for me to make sure we haven't missed anyone. There are families who will want to know."

Brett took the pen and paper. "Again. All of them?"

Shit, you'd think I was asking for a fucking grocery list. Lane took a long, slow breath. "Yes, please."

Brett looked at the ceiling, then down at the paper, and began to write. From time to time he would stop, count on his fingers or look at the door, concentrate, then continue to work.

Lane listened to the sound of the pen on the paper and the movement of the air coming from the vent above their heads. "At the end, please write down the total amount of money you scammed. Then we can talk about the drive-by in high school."

Brett didn't lift his head when he said, "I'm hungry. I want some food and another cup of coffee." He handed the list to the detective.

Just keep your cool for another couple of hours. Let him talk. Get it all down. Then you can get the hell away from him. "What would you like?"

"One of those Vietnamese beef subs and a big old cup of Tim Horton's coffee."

"And for dessert?" *Don't get sarcastic! You're not finished yet.* Lane managed deadpan.

"A vanilla milkshake would be nice."

Lane took the list, got up and went to the door. "I'll make the order." He opened the door, stepped outside and stood in the hallway. He used the thumb and forefinger of his right hand to massage the bridge of his nose.

Nigel came up beside him. "Want me to order his food?"

Lane nodded.

"What's the matter? Migraine coming back?"

Lane shook his head. "He just admitted to killing twenty-seven people and then ordered a sub, a cup of Tim's and a milkshake." He looked sideways at Nigel. "It's all the same to him. Killing is just like ordering lunch." He handed the list to his partner.

Nigel took the list of names. "Want me to take over?"

Lane took a couple of long breaths. "I'm not done yet." He opened the door and went back inside. *He wants the story out because he sees it as his legacy. Just let him tell the story.* "Food's on the way." He closed the door.

"I'm starving. You order, too. I hate eating alone." Brett looked up at Lane.

If I eat with you, food will never taste the same. "I'm not hungry. Let's keep talking until the food gets here. Who was with you when you did your first kill?"

"That guy killed one of our friends. He hit our friend over the head with a toilet seat. We went out and evened the score."

"We?" Lane felt the excitement rising up, a tension just inside the ribcage.

"Bertoulli, Rogerson and me."

"By Bertoulli and Rogerson you mean...?"

"Ben Bertoulli, the lawyer who just dropped me as a client, and Bill Rogerson, the solicitor general who won't take my calls. Rogerson drove, Bertoulli sat in the back seat and I pulled the trigger."

"The three of you kept in touch over the years since high school?"

Brett tipped his head from side to side. "We'd keep in touch from time to time. Then Ben saw an opportunity and decided we should go into business together with MCSC."

Keep your tone level. Don't lead him into his answers. Be patient. Wait!

"I had it figured out. If I invested in MCSC, I could live in Cuba with Sonja, have a steady income — I already have a house there — and forget about the winters. I just needed fifty thousand more. One more week and I would have gotten it." Brett looked at the door and then at Lane.

The detective frowned.

"Rogerson didn't invest directly. He's too smart for that. Bertoulli and me —" Mara pointed at his chest for emphasis "— agreed to give him a percentage in cash at the end of every year."

Lane had a flashback of the old woman picking up the phone at Bow Valley and beginning her one-sided conversation without entering a number. How vulnerable she was. He shook his head. *Just a bit longer. Keep focused.* "If you averaged fifty thousand per person you murdered, then that works out to one point three million."

"Except for the first guy, I didn't look at it as murder. I was doing the geezer a favour. You have to see it through my eyes. I saw the way they lived. If I ever get to be like that, I hope someone will do the same for me. Besides, I didn't kill everyone I scammed. There were lots of geezers who forgot about the money the day after the deal was done. After I made a bit of money I began spending more and more time in and around the Caribbean on holidays. Then I went to Cuba and met Sonja. Her family was pretty happy when we got married."

"You want to serve your sentence in Cuba?"

Brett laughed. "No way. Have you seen what a Cuban prison looks like? Besides, I won't live that long."

"Why do you say that?"

"The deal's already been made." He pointed his finger at Lane. "This is payback."

"What does that mean?"

"You're the detective. You figure it out. I'm tired and I'm hungry. I'm done for the day." Brett crossed his arms and closed his eyes. "I'll talk some more tomorrow."

✕

Lane walked alongside Nigel, who grabbed his partner's arm when Lane tripped over an uneven section of sidewalk on Stephen Avenue Mall. "You gonna be okay?" Nigel asked.

Lane shook himself, took off his sports jacket and slung it over his left arm. "The guy was telling me about what he'd done." Lane looked around to see if anyone was within earshot. "There was so little passion in his voice. It was all so matter of fact. So pedestrian." He looked around at the people sipping coffee, people pushing baby carriages, a man walking his dog (both owner and pet had round, flat faces), people checking their phones, a guy with a plastic bag leaning over a garbage can and pulling out a plastic bottle, a woman in red stilettos announcing her passing. *It's hard to get back to seeing the world as it is after an interview like that.* He turned to Nigel. "I never said thanks."

Nigel looked startled. The freckles on his cheeks were more pronounced when his face was tanned. "For what?"

"For seeing Brett when I walked right past him at Bow Valley."

"No problem." They walked up to Terri's coffee cart. "My treat."

"My mind was still fuzzy from the migraine."

"That's why we work together. We have each other's backs. What one misses, the other sees."

Terri looked over the espresso machine at them. "The usual?"

Nigel held up a ten and she took it in her right hand.

"We need to get back to Carlo and Anita about their grandmothers." Lane looked down along the avenue.

Nigel pulled out his phone and checked an app. "Carlo's a ten-minute walk away."

"You still have your copy of the confession?" Lane asked.

Nigel nodded and tapped his heart.

"Here you go, boys!" Terri handed over the cups and Nigel's change. They walked west along the mall until they crossed 5th Street and spotted Carlo as he swung open the awning and locked it in place.

Lane threw his empty cup in the trashcan, put his hand on Carlo's shoulder and felt the power in the man's muscles. "Got a minute?"

Carlo looked back and down at Lane. His dark hair was cut short. He wore a white T-shirt and black shorts. "You get him?"

Lane nodded. "It's not public knowledge, but he confessed to killing your grandmother."

Carlo nodded, then leaned his arm up against the side of the food truck and began to sob.

Lane's phone rang. He stepped back as he pulled out the phone. "Lane."

Lori said, "The uniforms found the motorhome just where Mara said it would be, but it was empty. The forensics team is on its way."

"Thanks." Lane hung up and waited for Carlo, who turned, wiped his eyes and nose with the sleeve of his T-shirt and looked at the detectives.

Nigel reached into his pocket and handed Carlo a tissue. The white disappeared in the man's massive hand as he worked to wipe his face, then moved closer and hugged them both. "I figured you guys would write my nana off." *I can't breathe! This guy is all muscle and marshmallow*, Lane thought. Then Carlo released them, saying, "Come on. I'm gonna feed you."

Fifteen minutes later, Lane felt optimism seeping back. He held half a calzone in his right hand. He watched a young woman in yoga tights hand her empty water bottle to a man wearing hand-me-down pants, shirt and shoes as he approached a garbage can. The man returned the favour with a toothless smile. Lane looked up at a clear blue sky and took another bite of Carlo's heavenly mix of fresh bread, tomato sauce, buffalo mozzarella and spiced meat. His phone rang just before Nigel's. They both fumbled for phones and read a text message from Lori. *We need you back now. Brett Mara is missing.*

Ten minutes later, they arrived at Lori's desk. She lifted her eyebrows, then said, "They found him."

Lane looked at Lori's face. *This is bad news.*

"At the bottom of one the elevator shafts." Lori raised her eyebrows. "They can't find the officers who were escorting him or the elevator repairman."

Lane lifted his chin. *A planned operation! Where are the tapes?* He turned to Nigel. "Check your computer to see if the Mara video is still there."

He turned to Lori, "Anyone been in our offices?"

She shook her head.

Lane pointed at her. "We need Nebal."

Lori lifted her phone to contact their trusted computer expert.

Lane stepped into his office and watched Nigel working furiously on his computer. He took a memory stick and attached it to his monitor.

Lane hung his jacket on the back of his chair.

"I've got it." Nigel wiped his forehead with his fingers.

"Make sure all of it's there." Lane reached into his desk drawer and pulled out another memory stick. "I want a copy too."

Nigel ejected his flash drive and attached Lane's.

Lane said, "Nebal is on her way. We need to get a copy of the files to Harper right away." *This will rattle the place down to its foundation.*

"What about the Po family?" Nigel asked.

"The priority is to secure the files first." Lane looked at his desk to see if anything had been disturbed.

Nigel said, "This is a mess and we have a power vacuum at the top. Looks like someone decided to take advantage of Simpson's leaving."

✕

They found Harper at the centre of the storm. His door was guarded by Jean, a five-foot-one, one-hundred-twenty-pound, silver-haired fifty-year-old secretary whom no one was prepared to mess with. The waiting-room chairs were filled with a pair of plain clothes RCMP, another pair from the Alberta Serious Incident Response Team and a pair of uniforms standing across the room from each other keeping an eye on the comings and goings. Jean pointed at Lane. "He wants to see you two right now!"

Nigel followed Lane past the heavy oak door and took in the room. He heard Jean shut the door behind them. Wearing his tie and dress uniform, Harper sat behind the desk. He held a phone in his right hand and waved with his free hand that they should sit at the coffee table.

Lane sat next to Nigel.

There was a knock at the door. Jean opened it and pointed at the coffee table. One of the uniforms placed three coffees in paper cups on the table and left. Lane recognized the cups from Terri's kiosk. He looked at the sides of the cups, saw one was labeled 'M' for moccaccino and helped himself.

"Okay. Will do." Harper hung up the phone, stood up, closed his eyes, leaned back and stretched his arms over his head. "Fuck!"

"Join us?" Lane asked.

Harper shook his head and smiled. "My first day as acting chief and there's a shit storm."

Nigel opened his mouth to speak. Lane stopped him by raising his eyebrows.

Harper sat down and stared at the cup in front of him. Then he looked at his former partner, shook his head and reached for his coffee. "We've got a dead prisoner and precious little else. I was hoping you two would have something so when ASIRT and the RCMP come in here, I'll have something to tell them."

Lane nodded at Nigel, who pulled the flash drive out of his inside jacket pocket. "Nigel made copies of our interview with Brett Mara."

Harper looked at the flash drive, his face turned red and he glared at Nigel.

Lane said, "I asked him to."

Harper reached for his coffee instead of the flash drive. "It's a procedural breach."

Lane nodded. "Mara confessed to twenty-seven murders. He also implicates Bertoulli and Rogerson as accomplices in one of the murders." Lane patted his coat pocket. "I have the signed list here. Nebal is in the process of backing up the video of Mara's confession."

"So Mara's killers are not aware of what he told you?" Harper sipped his coffee and closed his eyes.

Lane said, "Apparently not."

"That's something." Harper looked sideways at Nigel. "What have you got to say?"

Lane inhaled and waited.

Nigel said, "Rogerson, Bertoulli and Mara were up to their necks in this MCSC deal. When Mara got caught, they needed to shut him up. He got wind of it, talked to us first and screwed up their plan."

"So it's good news and bad news."

Lane tilted his head right and then left. "Depends on how you look at it."

"What do you mean?" Harper leaned forward and studied Lane.

"Mara isn't killing anymore, and we have solid evidence on two of the accomplices involved with Mara. And, if he's elected, Simpson may be the next solicitor general." Lane sat back and took a pull on his coffee.

"That still leaves a prisoner's body at the bottom of the elevator shaft. That's not going away." Harper looked at the ceiling as if seeing something up there for the first time.

Lane said, "Desperate people make mistakes. They shut Brett Mara up after we got the confession. That means we're a step ahead. Now all you have to do is let ASIRT and the RCMP do their jobs while we build our case against Rogerson and Bertoulli. Nigel has already started looking at some of the financials." Lane turned to Nigel.

Nigel blushed.

"What?" Lane asked.

"I've been meaning to talk with you about that."

"Oh shit." Harper rolled his eyes.

×

<LEAD-IN STEPHANIE OZDURAN> YYC News uncovered a series of shocking revelations today about a high-profile member of the Alberta legislature and his connection to a US-based corporation. Kari Hernandez has an exclusive report.

<CUT TO KARI HERNANDEZ FOR STANDUP> Alberta solicitor general Bill Rogerson is set to profit from the private member's bill he initiated last spring. Mr. Rogerson and his longtime friends, Brett Mara and Calgary defence lawyer Benjamin Bertoulli, are involved in a mutually profitable scheme to enable Mi Casa Su Casa corporation to operate in Alberta. This corporation specializes in large-scale facilities for senior care.

Mi Casa Su Casa faces a class-action lawsuit in California. Relatives of deceased MCSC residents maintain their family members were defrauded of their property and in some cases their life savings.

Lawyers representing the survivors argue MCSC is designed to defraud vulnerable seniors, particularly those whose intellectual abilities are compromised by diseases like Alzheimer's. More controversial, they say MCSC may be a front for organized crime.

According to documents we've discovered, Mr. Bertoulli and Mr. Mara were prepared to invest millions of dollars to establish seniors residences in Alberta in partnership with MCSC. An agreement between Mr. Bertoulli and Mr. Mara refers to monthly cash payments to Mr. Rogerson as part of a profit-sharing arrangement with MCSC.

Even more startling is a report that Brett Cameron Mara died today while in police custody. And as this broadcast was going to air, we received reports that Mr. Bertoulli and Mr. Rogerson have been arrested. Obviously there is much more to this story.

Back to you, Stephanie.

<LEAD-OUT STEPHANIE OZDURAN> Thanks, Kari. YYC News will follow this story as more information becomes available.

✕

The uniforms brought Bertoulli and Rogerson in separately. Both were accompanied by lawyers. Lane prepared to interview Rogerson while Nigel got ready for Bertoulli. Harper was already waiting to watch the interviews on separate monitors. Both suspects and their lawyers appeared unimpressed, constantly looking at their watches, the clients making jokes. Lane and Nigel watched the pairs on Lane's large monitor in their office. Nebal had set up redundant backup systems and extra levels of security to prevent tampering.

"So, we're agreed. We start off with the financial evidence to lull them into a sense of bored security?" Lane glanced at his watch. *It's ten minutes to ten. I should feel tired but I'm wired.*

"Then we hit them with Brett's confession where he implicates them and show them a copy of his list of twenty-seven victims. Then give them a minute to realize they will be forever linked to a mass murderer." Nigel kept his eyes on Bertoulli as he studied the man's body language. "If he deals first, you buy coffee tomorrow."

Lane nodded. "We stay calm, confident. Then we wait. The waiting will break them." Lane studied Rogerson, who leaned his head back against the wall and closed his eyes. "Let's get started."

An hour later, Rogerson was struggling to remain alert. His hair was still cut short but his round face appeared to have gained a few more lines since their last meeting. Rogerson's lawyer, Robin Blair, was about forty, wore black pants, a white blouse, black shoulder-length hair, red lipstick and a toothy bleached smile. She said, "There is nothing definitive in your evidence. Quite frankly, there is nothing here that justifies detaining my client."

It's not so much what she says but the way she says it. Her voice is filled with arrogant condescension. Lane made up his mind. *Now's as good a time as any.* He reached over and turned the laptop so that Blair and Rogerson could see it. "This interview was done this morning. It may address some of your concerns about evidence, Robin." He pressed the button Nigel had marked for him.

Brett Mara's smiling face is unfocused at first, then the pixels coalesce into a crisp image.

That guy killed one of our friends. He hit our friend over the head with a toilet seat. We went out and evened the score.

We? the recorded Lane asks.

Bertoulli, Rogerson and me.

By Bertoulli and Rogerson you mean . . . ?

Ben Bertoulli, the lawyer who just dropped me as a client, and Bill Rogerson, the solicitor general who won't take my calls. Rogerson drove, Bertoulli sat in the back seat and I pulled the trigger.

Lane closed the laptop, then lifted a crime-scene photograph from a blue folder. The picture showed a body lying on the seat of a car. The steering wheel was visible in the left of the frame. The neck of the headless corpse lay against the passenger-side arm rest. "His name was Stewart Kalyk."

Lane studied the reactions. Rogerson's face was a mask, though admittedly a pale mask. Blair held her hand to her mouth. Lane put the photo back in the file, stood up and said, "Perhaps you would like some private time to discuss your options. There is more to the Mara interview if you'd like to watch it." Lane stepped outside, closed the door, turned and looked up at the uniform, who stood six feet four, weighed about two twenty and looked to be about twenty-two. "They will probably request a private room. If they do —" Lane held up his phone "— text me, then accompany them and remain outside the door. If they want to talk, text me."

The uniform nodded, Lane glanced at his watch, then walked down to his office. Harper, looking more than slightly rumpled, was waiting there with Nigel. Lane asked, "Where's the Crown Prosecutor?"

Harper drank from a bottle of water. "On the way. He was pissed about the time until I told him what was up."

"Who is it?" Lane sat down and reached for another bottle of water. Someone had set a half dozen on his desk.

"Brown." Harper took a long pull from his water.

"That asshole," Nigel said.

Here we go! Nigel, couldn't you just leave it alone?

Harper choked, coughed, wiped his face and smiled, "Yeah, but he's our asshole."

Nigel pointed at Lane. "The odds are two to one against you."

Lane leaned forward and lifted his eyebrows.

Harper wiggled his thumb at Nigel, then at himself. "We both think Bertoulli will cave first."

When did the pair of you become buddies? Lane wondered. His phone began to vibrate.

×

Lane opened the door to the room where Blair and Rogerson sat shoulder to shoulder. The walls were grey, and Lane thought he detected some of that colour in Rogerson's complexion.

"Mr. Rogerson has agreed to address some of the allegations. He is willing to discuss the murder of Mr. Kalyk." Blair glanced at her client. She continued in the same arrogant, condescending tone. "He knows nothing about the murders of either Camille Mara or any of the patients under the care of Brett Mara."

Lane turned to Rogerson and waited. *Obviously they have prepared what he is about to say. Just wait and let him go ahead. After that, hit them with the ultimatum.*

Rogerson looked into the camera and said, "I was there the night Kalyk was shot. Brett and Ben told me that they wanted to scare Kalyk after what he did to our friend."

Lane held up a finger. "By Brett and Ben, you are referring to Brett Mara and Ben Bertoulli?"

Rogerson nodded. "That is correct. I pulled up beside Kalyk's car. He looked over and Brett shot him in the face. I knew Brett had a sawed-off shotgun, but he told me that it wasn't loaded."

Lane waited. *Let him finish his story.*

"When I got into politics, Ben and Brett approached me with the MCSC deal and wanted me to be a part of it. I refused. Ben told me that they would leak the information about the shooting and my involvement as the driver if I didn't go along with their plan." Rogerson looked past Lane and stared at the door. "When I told them that if they did that, I would reveal their involvement in the shooting, Brett said he would go after my family."

Lane nodded. "Did Bertoulli know about the plot for the Kalyk shooting?"

Rogerson nodded. "Yes."

"You will testify Bertoulli conspired to commit the Kalyk murder?"

"Yes." Rogerson looked at the camera.

"My client has lost his reputation and his career," Blair said.

Lane kept his tone even when he said, "You will also provide the names of other investors in MCSC."

Blair said, "That's not part of the deal."

Lane shrugged. "Then there's no deal. Mr. Rogerson will be charged with conspiracy."

Blair looked sideways at her client. "That's flimsy at best." Her tone had lost its arrogant certainty.

Lane watched Rogerson. *He heard it in her voice as well. When her plan has a glitch, she folds.*

Blair turned to Rogerson. "It's your call."

Lane watched Blair's eyes. *And she folds like a worn-out queen in a cheap deck of cards.* Lane maintained a nondescript expression.

"Do you have a pad of paper and a pen?" Rogerson asked.

chapter 17

\<LEAD-IN STEPHANIE OZDURAN> We have an update on the story that has shaken the premier's office and shocked many Albertans.

\<CUT TO KARI HERNANDEZ FOR STANDUP> Calgary is buzzing today after some shocking revelations about charges against a local lawyer and the province's solicitor general. At a news conference a few hours ago, Crown Prosecutor Stephen Brown announced that Calgary lawyer Ben Bertoulli and Alberta solicitor general Bill Rogerson are being charged with a number of offences, including accessory to murder for a decades-old drive-by shooting.

Brett Mara, co-accused in the charges against Mr. Bertoulli and Mr. Rogerson, was found dead in police custody. Police are saying little at this time, but the RCMP and the Alberta Serious Incident Response Team are investigating the death.

\<BACK TO STEPHANIE OZDURAN IN STUDIO> And there was a development involving multiple deaths in seniors residences?

\<BACK TO KARI HERNANDEZ, STANDUP> Yes. We have heard unconfirmed reports that Brett Mara has confessed to killing twenty-seven people, most of them seniors under his care at various facilities in the city. These deaths were often misdiagnosed as myocardial infarctions, better known in layman's terms as heart attacks.

Several Calgary families became suspicious when they discovered large withdrawals from their relatives' accounts immediately prior to their deaths.

\<LEAD-OUT STEPHANIE OZDURAN> Thank you, Kari. YYC News will update this story as it continues to unfold.

chapter 18

Lane sat up, swallowed to get some moisture in his dry mouth and looked at the clock. He squinted. "Ten o'clock. What day is it?" He got up and seven minutes later was in the shower.

Arthur was in his office working on a client's account as Lane went to the top of the stairs. He went into the office and put his cheek against Arthur's.

"You think I'm that easy?" Arthur asked.

Lane shrugged. "This case—"

"I know. We've been watching it on the news and reading about it in the paper. The kids have about a million questions, so be prepared for the interrogation when you finally get home for dinner. I've been handling things while you've been busy. Be ready, there've been some major developments. And Lane?"

"Yes?"

"What kind of shit storm have you walked into?"

Lane looked at the shiny top of Arthur's head.

"Do you really think these three guys were the only ones involved in the deal?"

Lane shook his head. "No." *Don't tell him about the list just yet.*

"Just watch your back."

Major developments? The doorbell rang. Lane's ride was waiting.

×

Lane set a cup of tea down on Lori's desk. She mouthed a thank you, then continued with her phone conversation. He walked into his office and set a coffee on Nigel's desk.

Nigel looked up, smiled and said, "I lost the bet. I'm supposed to be buying coffee. How did you know that Rogerson would deal first?"

Lane sat on the edge of his desk, set his moccaccino on the corner, then shrugged. "I just got the feeling he was tired of hiding and wanted to come clean. Bertoulli and Mara were using him and his position. They threatened to leak the information about the Kalyk shooting to pressure Rogerson into playing along. It looks like Bertoulli and Mara planned the killing and Rogerson was not in on the conspiracy. He gave the impression he was relieved when he told me about his role. Relieved the story was out and he didn't have to cover it up anymore."

Nigel sipped his coffee, then set it down. "Funny. I got the feeling Bertoulli could argue black was white and have me halfway convinced after five minutes. The guy is a compulsive liar. I figured he would be the first to spin some kind of yarn implicating everyone else."

Lane laughed.

"What's so funny?"

"He's kind of a caricature. One of those guys who is all hair and teeth and sells self-help advice."

"The bullshit never really stops with Bertoulli. I think he convinces himself he's telling the truth when he's lying."

Lane smiled. "Exactly."

Nigel's eyes opened wide. "I was supposed to remind you to phone someone in Havana."

Lane tapped his forehead with his open palm. "Deylis. I need to call her and let her know what's happened." He sat behind his desk and picked up the phone. "Without her help, Brett would still be out there and the people behind MCSC might have been able to go ahead with their plans."

"After you make that call, we need to head over to Phoenix Kitchens. I'll let them know we're coming."

×

Forty minutes later they passed through Inglewood, past coffee shops, restaurants and funky boutiques. Nigel was driving. "What did Deylis have to say?"

Lane looked out the window at Spolumbo's, known around the city for its sausages. "She was a bit shocked to find out how many deaths Brett was responsible for. And she seemed pleased to have played a role in the whole thing. She's going to get back to us with the details on Sonja's return."

Nigel turned south onto Blackfoot and drove under the railway bridge along the narrow lanes on their way up the hill. The view of downtown and the Stampede Grounds kept Lane's attention until Nigel turned left into Highfield Industrial Park. Nigel parked out front of Phoenix Kitchens next to the green metal garbage bin tagged with white graffiti. It took a minute to manoeuvre their way along the wooden planks leading to the temporary entrance, then upstairs. Heads turned from four desks set in four corners of the room. Samples of granite, cabinet doors and fixtures leaned against walls. Neville stood leaning against the door-frame of the private office. Aunt Rose stood beside him. Anita tucked hair behind her shoulders as she got up to greet the detectives. "You have news for us?"

Lane looked at Anita. "We came to thank you for the information that led to the arrest of the people responsible." He looked at each face in return, their eyes locked on his. He waited while Neville quietly translated for Aunt Rose before continuing. "Brett Mara was arrested and he confessed."

Aunt Rose kept her eyes on Lane and Nigel as she spoke to Neville, who asked, "My aunt asks why you refer to more than one person."

Lane nodded. "May I ask for an assurance that none of you will talk of this outside this office?" He made eye contact with each person in the room.

Neville spoke. Lane looked at Nigel, who said, "It's Mandarin. He's telling them to keep their mouths shut."

Neville said, "We promise."

Lane asked, "You will not talk to the media? There will be court cases. One of the men responsible is very slippery. You don't want him squirming out of prison."

Neville translated.

Aunt Rose spoke in Mandarin. Nigel translated. "She says we promised, now get on with it."

Lane said, "Brett worked with others who were planning to exploit seniors."

Aunt Rose spoke. Neville smiled. Nigel said, "She called them pigs."

Lane smiled at her. "The pigs will be facing various charges and it will be in the news."

Anita asked, "How did Ayah die?"

Lane said, "He smothered her."

Anita wiped at a tear as Neville translated. There was a howl of grief. Lane watched as Aunt Rose cursed, then pulled Neville closer. He said, "She thanks you and asks you to come with us."

Lane asked, "Where?"

Neville wiped his eyes with fingertips. "Rose wants to take you to a restaurant we know. She wants you to be our guests."

It took less than half an hour to reach the restaurant in Chinatown. It was nearly fifty metres from Centre Street and the Bow River. Lane walked alongside Aunt Rose up the long flight of stairs to the restaurant. He held the door for her. Inside, she took his elbow past the gold dragons guarding the entrance. They sat at a table in the corner of a room, which Lane estimated could seat over a hundred. Nigel was asked to sit on the other side of Rose. Anita was directed to order and by the time the first plate arrived, Lane was famished.

He was taking his second bite of garlic chicken when Nigel said, "Hey, Paul!"

Lane looked up. The room was half full. Nigel said, "Aunt Rose had them —" he pointed at Anita and Neville "— call everyone close to Ayah to come and celebrate her life." Lane looked around the room where waiters swam between tables, children sat on laps or in booster chairs, families chatted with one another.

Aunt Rose spoke. Nigel translated, "She says she thought Ayah's killer would never be caught because she's Asian and the police wouldn't look very hard."

Lane shrugged, "That thought never occurred to me."

Aunt Rose spoke; then Nigel said, "And that's why she invited us here." Nigel leaned back and pointed his chopsticks at Lane. "She says she wanted us to see this. Ayah touched so many lives." He lifted his eyebrows, adding that shit-disturber smile. "We have more than twenty families to notify. Do you think every notification will be like this?"

Lane shook his head. A feeling of intense satisfaction followed by dread. Ever since his mother took a belt to his back he'd been haunted by joy. Killing Pierce had amplified the feeling that every gram of joy inevitably resulted in a kilogram of pain.

chapter 19

Lane came into the kitchen wearing his blue suit and tie.

"Where are you going?" Christine aimed a spoonful of Pablum at Indiana's mouth.

"A memorial service." Lane popped a strawberry in his mouth. It was a tiny bomb of flavour. He closed his eyes to savour it.

Indiana took the spoonful of Pablum, then took his time to spit it slowly back out. Christine sat back, and hooked a bare toe over the rung of a nearby chair. "Dan's grumpy."

"How come?" Lane asked. He picked up another strawberry and popped it in his mouth.

"He and I want a place of our own." She looked sideways at her uncle to gauge his reaction.

His hand stopped with another strawberry about halfway to his mouth. He looked at Indiana, then back at Christine. *I don't want you to go.* He felt yesterday's joy spilling out. He looked at Indiana's light-brown hair, his green eyes and round cheeks, the Pablum oozing down his chin. A flashback struck with cruel intensity. He saw the back of Cori Pierce's head and the Glock in his hand. His stocking feet were thawing as the Jeep's heater fan blasted warm air onto the floor. Lane could feel the Glock in his hand as he stared at Cori's head.

"What do you think?" Christine asked.

Lane blinked, then looked at his right hand holding the strawberry. He looked at Indiana, who put his lips together and blew. Pablum sprayed onto the front of Christine's T-shirt and she cried, "Indy!" Lane watched her take a wipe from the blue package and rub it across the baby's face. He turned his head from side to side.

Lane put the strawberry back in the bowl. Appetite had deserted him.

×

Morning sunlight filtered through the stained-glass window of the funeral home chapel and illuminated the podium in a rainbow of colours. Lane and Arthur sat next to each other. Arthur smelled of soap and aftershave. He wore a dark-grey suit, mauve shirt and light blue tie. Lane picked a piece of white lint off his blue jacket, then lifted the creases on the knees of his matching pants. Arthur put his left hand over Lane's right. "You've been uptight all morning. We're almost there."

Corinne Bailey Rae's "Butterfly" began to play as Gloria walked up to the front. She was followed by her brothers, a niece and a nephew. A young man pressed a button on a laptop and a slide show began. Lane leaned back and turned his head to the right, anticipating the images like a physical blow. The first picture was of a stone-faced family with Gloria's smiling mother seated up front. Her children and husband stood behind her in the backyard. Gradually the pictures began to change. Gloria and her brothers grew into their teens and twenties. Their mother was relegated to one side or the other. More and more, as the years passed, the sons and daughter could be seen to smile. Gloria's mother was increasingly absent from the photos. The final image was of Gloria flanked by a niece and a nephew; all were smiling.

Lane felt Arthur touch his arm. "Did you see it?"

Lane looked at Arthur. "See what?"

Gloria's brother stepped up to the podium and said, "A tyrant can rule only as long as we let her. When we gather together and rebel, the tyrant's power is gone. That is the lesson of our family and of Christine, my niece. We are here to celebrate the survival of a family and the life of a child who was the catalyst for our rebellion."

The slide show began again from the beginning. Lane looked beyond the stone-faced group and to the top right of the frame. He focused on the window of his childhood bedroom. A shadowy, gaunt ghost child in a white shirt could be seen behind the glass. Arthur touched Lane's arm and pointed. "There you are."

At the end of the service, as Lane and Arthur tried to slip through the back doors, one of Gloria's brothers stopped them. "Hang on. Don't rush away. My brother and I wanted to say thank you."

Lane turned and faced two men. Both wore black jackets and open-necked shirts. They reminded Lane of their father, an ox of a man. The older brother shook Lane's hand, then said, "My sister needed this. She seems to be a little more at peace with what happened. Thank you."

The other brother shook Lane's hand, then turned to Arthur and shook his hand. "Thank you both for coming and for what you did to make this happen for Gloria."

Lane shrugged. "It's my job."

The lines on the older brother's forehead deepened. "You look pale."

"He saw his picture in the window," Arthur said. "It brought back some memories."

The youngest nodded. "'The ghost.' We used to call you that. We all worried about you because of the way your family mistreated you. But you're not a ghost anymore." He pointed at his brother. "We're not ghosts anymore either. Our mother tried to take our power away, but we ended up taking it all back. It looks like you got yours back as well."

"And more." The older brother smiled and handed Arthur a card. "You ever need renovations, you call us." Someone called out to the brothers, and they turned.

Arthur and Lane walked out into what remained of the morning. "Drop me off at the LRT station?" Lane asked.

When Arthur pulled into the parking lot of the Brentwood station, he said, "Before you go, we need to talk. Things have been happening at home while you've been consumed with this case."

Lane released his seat belt then turned to face Arthur. "Christine already told me about the condo."

"You need to know the whole story. It's been pretty intense at home for the last few days."

Lane took a deep breath. "What's Lola up to now?"

Arthur reached over, turning up the air conditioning. "Actually it's Dan and John who've been working things out. John came over to apologize for their leaving after the wedding in Cuba. Christine was blunt as only she can be. Then we all listened when John said he'd like to have a relationship with Dan, Indy and Christine. He explained how his daughter moved away because she and Lola butt heads. And he talked about how they haven't seen Linda in more than a year. Then Matt jumped in and said Christine needs to be treated better by John and Lola."

One of Lane's eyebrows lifted. "Matt stuck up for her?"

Arthur nodded, smiling. "Yes, and Dan agreed, which kind of made Christine happier."

"That's good." Outside movement caught Lane's eye. A man pushed a baby carriage with a sleeping infant under the shade of a canopy, a toddler perched on his shoulders. "What did you have to say?"

"Mostly I let them work it out."

"Really?" Lane smiled as he looked at his partner.

"I know. It was a struggle, but I figured my big mouth would only complicate matters."

"So it was John who came up with the condo idea?"

Arthur nodded. "Apparently. He said they had a condo looking for a tenant and he offered it to the kids rent-free as a kind of peace offering."

"No strings attached?" Lane shook his head remembering Lola pulling the strings in Cuba.

"He didn't use those words."

Lane inhaled then exhaled slowly. "It's really Christine and Dan's decision."

"I know. And Lola will always be a pain in the ass. But—"

"But what?"

"—she can only manipulate us if we let her."

"You're forgetting something." Lane opened the door.

"What's that?"

"Lola only goes along with what benefits Lola."

×

Terri handed him a moccaccino. "You look like shit again."

Lane tried to smile. "Actually, I believe I'm feeling better."

Terri shook her head as if to say *Don't bullshit me.* "It was you and the young guy who got that Mara asshole."

"Nigel was the one who grabbed him." Lane took a sip to see if it would revive him.

"Can't believe he killed that many people."

Lane raised his eyebrows, then shrugged.

"Anyway." She lifted her right hand. "Good job."

"Thanks." Lane raised his cup, then walked down the mall.

Five minutes later, Lori watched him as he walked into the office. She lifted a bottle of acetaminophen. "Got another migraine?"

"No, but thanks." He held his palm out as she dropped a couple of pills into it. "What's up?"

"Besides the fact that you're looking slightly spiffy today?"

"Spiffy?"

"That's what my dad used to call it when he got all dressed up."

Lane tried to smile.

"Harper asked to see you and Nigel when you got in. Want me to call and see whether he's available?" Lori reached for her phone.

"Sure." He stepped inside of the office, set his coffee down on his desk and hung his jacket over the back of his chair. He picked up his cup and went to the door. "Nigel around?"

Lori put her hand over the receiver. "In the little boys' room." She looked out into the hallway. "Here he is." She pointed at Lane and then toward the ceiling. "Off you go."

Nigel joined him in the hallway and they rode the elevator to Harper's office. Jean wore a white blouse and newly quaffed silver hair. "He'll be available in a minute." She was ten seconds off.

Lane and Nigel went inside and sat down at the coffee table. Lane looked at his coffee cup, then at the others. "Sorry, guys."

Harper waved his hand. "Not important." He didn't smile.

Shit. Bad news again, Lane thought.

"We found our elevator repair guy. A friend in the RCMP sent me this." He waved them over and pointed at a picture on his computer monitor. "The repair man was able to avoid every security camera but this one." The image revealed a man with dark hair mostly concealed by a grey ball cap. He wore a jacket with ELEVATOR SERVICE written across the front.

"Sean Pike," Lane said.

Nigel looked at Harper, then Lane. "Who?"

"Brother of Stan Pike." Harper said.

"This means the killing of Mara was an inside job," Lane said.

"He's a cop?" Nigel asked.

Harper nodded. "I was wondering who would take over Moreau's operation. It looks like Pike's been anointed."

"Pike's on the MCSC list we got from Rogerson. Do the RCMP have him in custody?" Lane asked.

Harper shook his head. "Pike's in the wind."

Lane asked, "You saw the list?"

Harper nodded.

"You saw Fuentes there, then."

Harper said, "That's right."

"Fuentes?" Nigel asked.

"From Mexico. Has connections with the UN gang in Vancouver. Looks like he's expanding," Harper said.

"Where does that leave us?" Nigel asked.

"Good question." Lane took the last pull from his moccaccino.

×

After they left Harper's office, rode the elevator down and stepped out onto the main floor, Nigel looked at Lane's cup, then asked, "Want another one?"

"That would be great." Lane tossed the cup in the office garbage can while Nigel turned and headed out onto the street.

Lane walked into his office. Lori's chair was pushed up next to the keyboard and her sweater hung neatly on the chair's back. *She's gone for lunch.* He took the keys from his pocket, opened the door to his office, took off his jacket, hung it behind the door and sat down behind his computer. He looked at the tiny tape recorder on his desk, reached into the drawer and pulled out a pair of new batteries. He took the old ones out, dropped them in his drawer and put the new batteries in. Then he opened his computer and looked over the map they'd created for the Mara file.

There was a knock on his open door. He looked up and saw Lola dressed in a grey business pantsuit. A white crocodile handbag hung over her shoulder. A red silk scarf was wrapped around her neck. "Hello, detective."

What are you doing here? Lane nodded. "Hello, Lola." He got up as she closed the door, then stood with her back to it. He sat back down. He fought the anxiety making his nerve endings tingle and his belly clench. He glanced right, spotted the tape recorder, reached over and switched it on.

"I wanted to speak with you about my grandson." Lola put her right hand across her chest to hold the straps of her handbag.

Lane inhaled. *I've just heard confessions from a serial killer and the former solicitor general. Why does she intimidate me?*

"John and I have spoken, and we feel that Dan, Christine and Indiana need a place of their own."

"That's what you've decided?" Lane adopted his interrogation voice out of habit. *Here it comes.*

"We offered them one of our condominiums rent-free."

Lane waited. *You knew yesterday's joy would be followed with something like this.*

"I've been concerned for Indiana's safety because of your work. Matt was kidnapped as a result of your choice of profession, and you must agree that Indiana's safety is a priority. It's best for them if they have a safe place to raise their family." She lifted her chin. "And I have some very personal concerns."

"They are?"

"My grandson is growing up in the home of a killer." She raised her open hand again, expecting opposition from Lane.

He inhaled slowly and focused on her eyes. *Is she nuts?*

"Of course what you did was legal, but I think you will agree — if you look at the situation dispassionately — that Indiana's psychological needs would be better served in an environment free from the inevitable aftermath of such an event. Besides, he needs a more traditional family environment." Lola waited before asking, "Have you anything to say?"

The door opened, it hit Lola in the backside and Nigel's head appeared. "Sorry."

Lola turned, opened the door wide, looked over her shoulder at Lane and said, "It's for the best." She walked past Nigel and was gone.

Nigel stepped into the office with three cups in a pressed cardboard tray. "Sorry about that. I didn't know you had someone in here."

Lori appeared behind Nigel. "Who was the woman with the Gadino?"

"Gadino?" Nigel asked as he set the tray on his desktop.

"The white handbag with the white diamonds. Do you have any idea how much one of those costs?" She looked at Lane.

He shrugged, reached for the tape recorder, shut it off and asked, "How much?"

Just carry on as if nothing's happened. He felt a deep sense of emptiness. *Does Lola have a point?* Fatigue crashed upon him.

Lori said, "Over thirty thousand dollars."

"Is that all?" Lane said. *Lola, who else have you been persuading?*

ACKNOWLEDGEMENTS

Doctors Bruce and Navaid, thank you.

Thank you to the amazing people at Pages Books on Kensington for supporting local writers.

Again, thanks to Tony Bidulka and Wayne Gunn.

Mary, Alex and Sebi, thanks for the suggestions and feedback.

Thank you to the kind staff at Iberostar Playa Alemdeda in Veradero, Cuba.

Matt, Jenna, Natalie, Leslie, Claire, Jason and Cathy: thanks for all that you do. In particular, thank you, Leslie, for the way you painstakingly edit and refine the novels to create an infinitely improved story.

Detective Dave Sweet, your information is invaluable.

Thanks to creative writers at Nickle, Bowness, Lord Beaverbrook, Alternative, Forest Lawn and Queen Elizabeth.

Sharon, Karma, Luke, Ben, Indiana and Ella. Every day I feel fortunate to be part of this family.

In 2004, Garry Ryan published his first Detective Lane novel, *Queen's Park*. The second, *The Lucky Elephant Restaurant*, won a 2007 Lambda Literary Award. He has since published eight more titles in the series. In 2009, Ryan was awarded Calgary's Freedom of Expression Award. He currently lives in Calgary.